Lynn Buckle was born in the UK and after much travel has spent the last thirty years in Ireland. She is a successful Kildare based artist, tutor and writer. She spent years stealing feelings and painting them onto canvas, but her stories needed words and she changed to writing verse.

The Groundsmen is Lynn's debut novel.

With Best Wishes

Lynn Buckle.

Lynn Buckle

The Groundsmen

époque press

Published by époque press in 2018
www.epoquepress.com

Typeset in Minion Pro Regular/Italic &
Goudy Old Style Regular/Italic by **Ten Storeys**®

British Library Cataloguing-in-Publication Data.
A catalogue record for this book is available from the British Library.

ISBN 978-1-9998960-2-7 (Paperback edition)
ISBN 978-1-9998960-3-4 (Electronic edition)

MIX
Paper from
responsible sources
FSC® C018072
www.fsc.org

Dedicated to
Sr Reginald

The
Groundsmen

Cassie

The first hole that I dig in the garden is not very good, just a little hollow dug out of the grass with a metal spoon. White birds in Scotland do that in the winter snow to hide from the wind. I saw it on telly. They can even change colour. But I don't want to turn green so I just put things in the ground instead. Like the TV remote control. Grown-ups always want to control it, even me. I lie it down and put spoonfuls of mud over it, one at a time until it is covered. It looks like a TV remote covered in mud. I have to stab the ground and pull at it to get to the soft stuff underneath. There are grubs and they are grey. They are allowed to live in the cairn I am building. It is only a small wee thing of a mound. I will get better at it.

Louis

Me and Toby have been watching the match and our analysis of the post-match analysis is over so we can stop shouting at the TV instead of shouting at each other. And resume. We've talked it out and back again and then some more, in our heads at least, until the wife 'just nipping upstairs,' forgets to come back down again and we are left in our comfy silence to say what we really mean by saying nothing at all. The kids have been milling around the house finding comfort in the Sunday afternoon routine of adults in front of the TV and the freedom to do as they wish when the drinking gets to just past half-time time and there's nothing to do in the village because everyone has died and gone inside or never lived here in first place because it's such a boring place. They say. Half the houses in this estate are derelict, unfinished, in limbo while the rest were filled just in time with commuters like us who couldn't afford to buy in town when the Tiger was roaring. Not if you were yearning to buy everything else. The holiday, the wide-screen, the new kitchen every year and a sofa to go with each change of curtains to match the lick of paint. Caught in the slipstream. Caught in the side stream. She likes that wallpaper with over-sized flowers. It's an Art Deco look, she calls it. Liver and onions. And instead of buying bespoke furniture like her grandad made that lasts a lifetime she gets this expensive mass-produced reproduction shit so she can live out her dream of living in Downtown Abbey while living in a box the size of their boot room. We're just one step away from being better than we really are and never will be. We moved here when I got the promotion but she never stopped going on about moving back into the centre of town, says that's why she's depressed, doesn't know anyone anymore. It's only a bus ride in, I tell her, but you'd think it's a foreign country out here.

'It is,' she says, 'you can't understand a word the women are saying in their growling bogger accents.'

But it's got some cracking pubs, one for every twenty of the population. The other eighty are squeezed into Foleys of a Sunday night with a lock-in till five in the morning and God knows these fellas work hard on the farm, they deserve the break. And who cares if we talk a different language, no-one can hear a bleeding word anyway, not if it's any good, and the birds are all the same whether they're up for it or not. You don't need fancy talk for that when it's party time and there's vodkas. Hey I'm buying. A bit of skirt. It's deadly then down here but she never sees it in a good way. She just complains that at weekends everyone disappears for their sister's wedding or to have roast dinner at their Mam's because they still haven't learnt how to cook at the age of thirty-five. That makes us old on Sundays with our mothers passed away and a slumping grumping fourteen-year-old doing our heads in. I put a vinyl on the turntable for some Led Zeppelin and air-drum my way through being seventeen again.

Toby

Heading for the kitchen for more beers and I see the fridge and pause because I'm thinking and I'm moving and there's all this in my way and I'm very nearly sinking, is it cheating if I'm holding onto chairs? They might trip me, hit me. Ladder-back stares. And shit you did that on purpose. Fuck, get back on track. Timing and winding in and out and carrying out the carry-outs and turn and say, so clearly now, I'm nearly now, so sober, I'll be needing another drink,

'Cally, want another beer?' keeping in with the sister-in-law.

'She'll have gone to bed for a read,' says Louis, all-time-prick-of-a-brother just because he's there, with that wiry hair, needing me and pleading for me. The snivelling golden child. We work together, almost live together, squeeze out the bloody blood-brother thing. An accidental death at work left him my accidental supervisor, by his accidental birth and they chose him instead of me or anyone at all, and still I have to run things for him, steering from behind while staring at his nodding head. Hating that head for having to pull those strings so that his mouth will open at the corner and tell me what to do. Telling myself. Like a ventriloquist I turn him around and he speaks, relays my instructions, elaborates on my ideas, delivers my reports, takes home my pay. To my family. He's in my way yet it's my duty to protect him still, lest they pick on him in the yard and I hear them jeering and turning in on him, feeble and waiting to be saved, he knows he will be. We know all this and we've never known it enough to stop it because if we did the sky would fall in. But we kick at it sometimes, annoyed, and carry on. So when he tries to tell me what to do without me telling him we both know where it will end and we don't go there for too long. So I can relax and do my thing, knowing he will do my thing too. And Cally does jack shit. Recalcitrant wife hiding in bed, inside a book. Sent there by a nun from school who hid rather too much under her habit and passed it on to her, a lifetime of reading Greek myths and legends while ignoring the real ones she lives with. Actually looking after them? Now that would be below her. What were her parents about, calling their fucking child Calypso for fucks sake? And then she keeps the nonsense going with Andromeda and, what is it? I can't even remember Cassie's real name. I mean, thank god you can shorten them down even if it does make them sound like boys. Kids all over the place and no dinner in the gaff, no point to Cally's existence. Get her out and get a new one, I would. I did. I got divorced from the baggy seagull. Not that Cally is. With her figure, and making the effort sometimes with her appearance, she must be up for it. Not with Louis though, he's too scrawny to be an egg and two rashers man, she needs a real man like me to show her what she's missing. But even she's getting on and, really, you know that underneath it all she's going to have that crêpey cleavage skin which takes two hours to unfold in the morning and a face that looks shit with a trolly-load of makeup on and shit without it. Our towels were always covered in that crap, the wife plastered in it and too much of a slattern to wash it off properly. Didn't even know what the word meant. And her legs shaved only to the knee, for crying out loud. And that smell coming off her, off all the women. You know they're on and you have to say, 'pretty woman,' not 'you stink woman,' and pretend while they go on about their daintiness and can't lift the sofa, the bag of coal, or change a tyre while they're rotting the room for the rest of us, while we're waiting for them to put out so we can put it in so they can act put out. Can't think when they turned into such witches. Maybe they were like it from birth and we just didn't know it. They disguised it well until they grew up into cackling gangs of legs and tight tops and I know what you got I don't need it spelt out you know that, you slag, so you clearly just want a fuck.

There's the boner. See what I mean? Just sit it out here with a can, and the wonderful lack of sound at the kitchen table with a view through the door of the match highlights on mute, and the satisfaction of a silent beer and a hard-on.

Cally

I lie on the duvet to stall the spinning, when really it's splurging and it's nothing like turning because the lying down never stops it. It's just something I do when it's finally too hard appearing normal and hiding it is harder. If anything it makes it worse, that makes me noble. If I could just stop my need to stem my lack of sobriety then I wouldn't feel confused and out of myself. I'd just be drunk. The cross I bear. So I hold on and concentrate on sitting it out, lying it out and drink less the next time. Think about sleep, even though I won't. About getting a lie-in tomorrow, even though I won't. About getting help. Ditto. Doing everything. Again. The laundry, the shopping, the food. No time for reading. Just writing a list of ham, milk, dinners, chipped tooth, new floors, a man out to fix the shower and the hole in the wall where he got mad, the stain on the wall where I got mad back, the drips of paint all around the tops of the walls where I had to decorate and I did it bad on purpose because he's too stingy to pay someone. He did after that. And too lazy to be a man and do it himself or to look after our little Cassie, or to make dinner, to make a worry list in the first place. Overdrive until it drives me mad and my jaw aches from not saying it. Have the kids eaten? A little gap in the day. Memory gaps getting bigger and hurting to fill them in. They must eat enough to get that size. They're skinny. My genes and his. They're bound to be. And short, because we are. Justified. Not ginger though. Not like next door. Neighbour never guessed which ones aren't his. And bloody Louis won't stop saying they don't look like him at all. How many times does one idiot need to say that to the other? I guess it suits him not to guess. Maybe too many for him to know which one is the father when any one of her customers could've had her. The two of them and their carry-ons. It's always the ugly ones end up having all the affairs. You'd think it would be the other way around. Thought he'd be grateful just to have got me. Stretching the skin around my skull to try and understand it. But this I know, he bangs her every Friday night after work. Tells me he's having a McDonalds on the way home. Likewise I don't mention it. Can't prove it so why bother going through all that drama, that shame, that bit of the world where separated people go to and can't come back from because you can't invite them round to a barbeque. They steal husbands and eat children. Or is that child maintenance? No, I don't want change. Comfort in foreverness. Forever and again until I die. I didn't know that it would be like this. No buzz or feeling sick with love, no lust pulling at my stomach, no chasing Eros to the ends of the Earth, no task too hard to find him. I won't feel any of that again. Or, if he can, so can I. Being bothered with that too though, so I stick with him. Applause. Until I look at him and remember he's just too ugly to fancy and I wonder when I stopped or, rather, when I happened to start noticing. His back is speckled. Not with acne anymore but some skin disease and a permanent joining of freckles and moles and growthy things which catch your hands as they rub over them. Sadness at the end of gliding over a taut body. And his vile palms which I flinch from, black scales flaking onto sheets, squeezing pustules until they've scabbed and he picks at them again until they bleed. Does the same to his feet. Turning into a lizard. His dry rot infecting everything.

'Andi. Andi? Can you give Cassie some dinner?' But not that.

Andi

'I gave her chips,' I tell Mum.

No answer. Ever. And thank you too. For feeding your kid. And getting her dressed. And breakfast and lunch and every damn bath and home-work and collecting her every day in between my own home-work and going to school and doing the washing and the drying and the putting away and getting bread and you're so flipping lazy you're almost dead. Why don't you just get out of your imaginary world of ancient stories? Get up and stop sleeping all day? It's your fault. Why don't you stand up to him? For us? Your job to do that. Andi, Andi, yes-I-will-love-your-kid-for-you-Andi-pandi-on-a-string-of-stars. I'll have to cycle to work later. And no lights in the dark. Bad hair after that. Repairing it again in the back of the shop, squeezed between crates as the lads take their chances at having a quick grope. The dopes. I'm imagining my hair straighteners burning their hopes as they hope to deflower me. The idiots. Like I'd let them in my box.

I open my cupboard, not that one, to look through my things and find it's open and that's the trouble. Some sins have occurred. I would never leave it like that. I check it, like, three times when I leave the room. Just in case. And then I go back to check it once more. Annoying, I know, but it's the door's fault, securing my insecurities. So someone has been in here. The hangers have gone all hay-wire and I think of the turmoil if I had a shed-full of grass like a farmer. The trouble I'd have tidying it into lines of furrows and furlongs, to get neat little shrines of orderliness. I have to keep my clothes on the floor in case I ruin the storage spaces. Need them for my mind. Only gifts and wings are allowed in here. A heavenly place for fear. But the intrusion has disrupted my comfort. Zone in on the ruin and what did they want? I want to know who? Who did this?

'Cassie. You've been in my room.'

Cassie

The fun of the scare when Andi chases me everywhere, I know she's just playing and I love it. Hiding from my sister and running full-speed, I like that she likes me and gets what I want. When she shouts she is funny, nothing like Mammy, and I run down the stairs to the sofa. Thwamp onto the cushions. Good sound. Again, off, jump, thwamp. Again, off, jump, thwamp. Again, off, jump, thwamp. Daddy says,

'Shut the fuck up.'

Again, off, jump, thwamp.

'Shut the fuck up,' he shouts.

He's hurting my arm. I get past him and hide at the other end. I'm fast. Yeah. In the hidey hole. Can't get me. Ow in my elbow pit. Stop pulling my arm out. Kick you, you. He pulls me in front of the fireplace. I watch white bits spitting at me from his face. My, what big teeth you have. All the better to taste you with. I go into a ball and

14

my snappy arm sticks behind me because Daddy makes it. I watch his froth fall down and sparks from the red coals land around me. They turn black. Burning smells and cracks he yanks. It's hot. They're both the same. I squeak then count to twelve to go away. Somewhere else. Someone will come soon. They will. They will. They will. Will they give it to me list. All the things I want list. Argos catalogue. Barbie car. Sylvanian caravan. Princess Ava tent. My Little Pony, the purple one. Mousy game. They will. Hello Kitty everything. Will. Will. Will. Andi is in. Frees me. She says,

'She's not a pig spit.'

And no I'm not, not a pig. And he did spit, but not like boys at school. Andi pulls me too but I'm not being punished, just pulled into our garden. Under no sun. And nothing new. To bury it.

Louis

The empty room is left full of something, gnawing at me it is. Not Cassie's vacant patch, bitch spawn for doing that, no it's the chasm around my desk at work. Around things unsaid, that were never seen. She said, he said, she saw, see-saw. It's all the bleeding time. So much of it. There's a pressure in the sides of my eyes. It runs through a semicircular piece of wire in my head and makes my teeth mad at each other. Can't do anything about that. So I look for lardy boy Toby. He's at my kitchen table again. How many babies did you raise? None. Exactly. So you don't know what it's like. You're still a kid then, playing at grown-ups. So don't be judgemental, because one day you'll learn and get a landing when you're handed a screaming rubber thing covered in blood and you can't think where it came from 'cause you'll never go back in there if you did and the screaming never stops, it just plays on in your head and they're all screaming at you all of the time. But not you Toby. You are free from that, relieved from that by a wife who couldn't have children, or didn't want your children and that's why she left you? Or she found out who you are and didn't like you. I know you and I don't like you. Hanging on to what you were over forty years ago. Instead of forgetting it you're still making it and faking it, the cool hard-nut. But guess what, I grew up too, and I can do all those things now. You're not three years older anymore and telling me to stay back to wait in the brick-walled alley in line with the other kids shuffling up to you to pay up and have a look at her and for fifty pence more get a feel or sometimes just because you're mean make me feel you too but it's free when we're in bed together and I like it, you tell me, and I want to be like you so I do. Only afterwards you treat me like shit like it's my fault so it must be. So you pretend you separated for something else, anything rather than this.

'Bro, pass us that beer,' he asks.

Twat, fecks sake, dick. Teeth getting tighter. Sidey eyes.

'What you doing?'

'Nothing.'

Andi

Chilly. Mum. Would. Say. Left out. Left standing. In the cold. Night air. Autumn grass. Be ready. Another chase. Alert to see. Everything. Checking vitals. Scanning. Nothing. Moves. In stillness. Still nothing. Double checking. Just waiting. Let the breath out. At last, longer breathing. Both of us inhaling and exhaling, steadying. Hanging on and listening to our own heavy heaving. Watching our breathy clouds, lit from indoors. We cup our hands to capture the magic misty balls. Cassie is down on all fours. I pretend that one of my exhalations is a ball of light, to see if she will catch it. She leaps up for it like a dog.

'Pat me and I'll make a dog breath,' Cassie says.

I play along and ask to see if dogs can breathe bigger than children.

'Sooo big,' she spreads her arms wide, 'planet-sized.'

Her globe of steam rises to the sky. We watch it with

our necks bent right back, waiting for collisions in the universe. As it fades we focus on the dots above, 'there's my constellation of stars, named after me,' I tell her. She doesn't get where I am pointing, pretends that she does, 'Andromeda. In another month you'll see shooting stars come out of it.'

'Why do you shoot stars out? Are they like those ants that had wings that got thrown out in the summer and died on the stones? When you throw stars out you die. Don't throw yours out Andi. I don't want you to die.'

I tell her I won't.

'If you do, can I have your butterfly wings to wear? Not the purple ones. The pink ones?'

'Yeah okay,' weird kid.

'What happens to all the boxes and bags when people die?' Cassie asks.

'What bags?'

'You know. Like if when you die, what will happen to your bag in your room and those two boxes in your wardrobe with stuff in?'

'You mean, what happens to people's things when they die?'

'Mmm.'

'People write down all the stuff they have and write a list of all the people they want to give it to and it's called a Will.'

'A will-you-give-it-to-me-list, like Birthdays?'

'Yeah, you freak.'

'Thanks. And will-you-give-me-your-butterfly-wings?'

'Alright, I said. Is that why you were at the boxes in my wardrobe and going through my things?'

'I was just hiding stuff for Blackie and looking for the things you-will-want-to-give-me.'

'Who's Blackie?'

'Me. He's our dog. He buries bones.'

'Not in my wardrobe he doesn't. You're not to go in there. I told you that. It's mine.'

'I didn't look in the boxes. I just wanted to look at them.'

'Very accurate excuse. Just don't. It's safe to go back in now.'

Toby

'Daddy, Andi's going to die,' that kid Cassie screaming, she is, coming into the kitchen.

'Jesus wept,' is the best you'll get out of Louis.

'Are you going to make her fall out of the sky?' Cassie asks her Dad.

'Tempting. But no. What you on about?' he replies.

Like, why does he bother to engage with that?

'Stuff I know,' says the brat.

'How would you know anything?' he's a fine one to talk.

'Kids and dogs know everything.'

'What? Who says?'

'Blackie.'

'Who's Blackie?'

'Me. I'm a dog. And I'm called Blackie.'

'So tell her to shut up then.'

Good man your-self. He turns to me and explains that

she is a dog that doesn't even exist.

'Like Orthrus,' I say, knowing he won't even get it.

'Sounds like a wart.'

'Or a woof.'

'No I'm Blackie,' she cries.

We ignore it.

'Jesus,' Louis exhales, looking at me like it's my fault she's weird.

You can see he's becoming patronising, getting above himself and the rebelliousness is kicking in. Squash it fast, don't let anything come out. Strangle the stupid whinging baby. Pretend everything's okay. Quick. Think of something nice. Cally. Oh yeah nice one, Cally in my head. Cally in the bed. She's lying up there now waiting for me to give her the shagging of her life because you can't do it for her. I'll sit here thinking of doing her and you're too weak to do anything about it. You're mine and she's mine. He'd probably let me too.

'Huh. Kids, hey?' I smile at him and think of brick walls.

'Yeah aren't they great? Imagination and all that,' he replies, bitter between the lines and returns the smile. Invisible like lemon juice ink. Heat it up and it'll all come out. He redirects his bile.

'Where's dinner, Cally?' he shouts, but it's all for show, she's a no show.

He gives Andi some cash and tells her to get us a Chinese, squeezing her as she passes, thinks I don't notice. But she says she's going to work now and we both offer to take her.

I tell him I'm heading that way anyway, might as well drop her off. Great to have her in the car, to be next to her. Those huge breasts sticking out into the windscreen. Asking for it, oh God how brilliant, footie, beer, tits so massive in my mind I'd burst. Instead I smile and keep it normal. I'd be doing her a favour after all. For Christ's sake, I love her, I'd never do that. Deciding which one of us will take her and which one of us will take her. Always get our way. We're hard. If I can just get out now, or if he can. But she's getting her bike out of the shed. We think of the bike with that seat between her legs, and we see her screwing down on it, wanting us instead. Don't say you never thought it. At least there's Cally in bed waiting for us. Rocks' agony. Two brothers.

Louis

'Best see if Cally will get us something,' to eat or to screw?

Looking at her lying flat-out in the bedroom and thinking I'll get her in her sleep. Her pile of books gets more of a fingering than I do. I could roll her over onto her side and slide it in before she notices and wakes up screaming help stranger getting me, I want you, rip me open. Please I'm wet for you, 'oh you're awake,' even better. She's asking for a gang bang. Pull her hands together and tie her up. Instead I say, 'you look nice there, mind if I join you?' easy does it now, don't want to scare her off. Flattery and all that fluff, makes her good to go. Go to for some relief. I can't stand the bitch, alright? Now make her think it's her idea. Don't touch her yet. Two minutes should do it, of lying on my back with a cock rock hard and a rack sat next to me of passive what-is-the-point-of-it lard. Letting one more minute pass, for the sake of decency. You're destroying me,

24

get a move on. Get a mower on that landing while you're at it. Start her off now and pretend she is some other beauty. That she never was. She's moving a bit. Like a jelly. She must be ready if she's squirming away from me on the bed and letting me stroke the leg. Safely up and down, working it until she comes around and her thighs are nearer to what I'm getting into and it's easy if she wants to, just stroking and blowing until she wants a bit but then she frowns. I tell her I'm only being friendly, that's all. Got away with it but not in there yet. She's playing dumb and slow, pretending she doesn't want to know. When really she's dying for it, really wants a dick in her hole in the car park in her stilettos with everybody watching her running away naked but really it's her signal just to give her one, 'mmmm you smell so good and so soft, you're gorgeous,' as if! And hey this is working, she isn't pushing me off, 'let me kiss you,' come on, 'just one kiss, please,' for feck's sake, you twat, you know you want it, 'darling,' Jesus, slow cow. She only needs six old men, really old now, to hold her down in the car park. One on each corner. One OAP does her and she whimpers and the really ugly one cums in her face and the fat one on top pounding away squealing and she can't stand it, as I'm watching her and I'm wanking as I'm wanting to do him too because I hate him because he's hot and he's not what I'm supposed to be fancying. I'm her, 'I really want you. Do you want to, you know?' damn I shouldn't have asked, I should just do it, 'turn over so I can rub your shoulders, just a massage,' fat fool always falls for that, 'isn't that nice?

You're very tense,' as I ready to aim lower each time as I circle down her body. She won't notice a thing. Nice and slow. Round and round, like the bike, I go. Pushing saddles right up inside. Smells of my old Uncle Brown as he does my backside. I mean to do hers. Because he's mean and I'm crying my eyes out and begging him to stop so she will cry her eyes out and beg me to stop. And we're wet for it. Let's see if she really is. Oh God, yes, she agrees to have sex! Tease her now, get her panting. Little finger, leave her waiting. For the big one. She is moving up and down. Happy days as I imagine you putting your pussy in the old man's face now aren't you? 'say you love me,' rubbing all over his wrinkly nose, 'beautiful,' and you hate it and it's great that you're splitting, 'let me inside you,' you stretchy old bag, 'you're a grand lass,' you tramp, you naughty, dirty, disgusting hag. Little boy, what a slag. Push down on your front and squash those tits back in, press them with weights till you're flat under-board. Bored by your buxomness. Bite them right off, 'your breasts are so nice,' for smashing, 'please, I want you so much,' nearly there. I nearly fancy women. This will show them when they stare, laughing at the limp one at the end of the line. I can get it up anywhere, screw this woman of mine. From behind. I have to get harder. I think of Uncle Brown coming down on my parts. One, two, saddles and ram them in. I shout, she shouts. She likes it, I tell her. The old man is laughing. I'm in Uncle Brown's hut as he dresses me in an outfit of a skirt and white socks and tells me I'm pretty and then I submit. The bastard, the deviant, the miscreant monster of mine. Uncle Brown buggery and suck it show time. Trying to get it in her for him, for causing that pain, banging her now because he's doing it again. For making me horny for making me sore, she'll pay for him wanting me, 'how lovely,' I say, pulling her apart. God why does she act like I'm breaking her heart and then she just lets me do it anyway? Look at him in there, tearing me asunder, and her not even noticing. Uncle gets cross and I get a punishing. Now that's a waste of a ride on you woman. At least pretend you love the men ruining your arse boy wonder woman, 'tell me what you want,' when we both know what you want, to be bent over old Uncle's lap, slap, and stick in you and I can see that you love it and recover from it like I did, so we open our mouths and have it rammed down our throats till we gag and he cums.

'I'm going to cum.'

What a slag.

Because my Uncle said I am.

Cally

Doing it with the vile stink of his curried-sweat, fag and beer breath, his rotten teeth on mine. I freeze in revulsion as his hands scratch over me with his infected bits, leaving me disgusted. And contracted. Waiting in a dark room and over to the right. Remembering something from long ago. When night-time kisses meant more than that and I curled under furls of blankets twisted, my only defence against sinister ways of living with a family too close and getting in bed with me and my sisters. He stands in the doorway, silhouetted. Seeing that sight, and I'm back in black and pain-coloured smells of trying to tell but no words came out. It's the same tonight. Not being able to say no because I couldn't say no because I didn't know, how to say it. I was small. Still can't. Still am. It means I'm never nearly there. Him the bitter runt, he laughs about putting paper bags on my head but really that's what I need to block him out so that I can make love with a gentle man. I have to think of Milton's face. That's the man I imagine, with a magic smile. He's tall and clean, has a mellow musky smell with a touch of mint and his broad shoulders hold it all back for me and carry it all for me, my emotional Samson. Crush me but you never will. We are in our own electric force field and he is close against my back. I feel his warmth on my neck, his beautiful hard wide mouth not quite touching, synapses reading pheromones, sensing the love and leaning in to savour it, wanting to give everything to each other, for each other. He loves me and I love him we murmur to each other, whispering our amazement softly. Each stroke of tenderness eases something beautiful down through my head and back into him again as we give and give and give to each other. Our bodies take over. The speed of physical need, in sensate sensations, to please. After we are both so full that we have to explode, we lie sated and waiting, unable to move. When we do roll into each other to cuddle the last niceness out of it, I see the kindness pouring from his eyes.

But then I see him.

'That was nice…if you had been there too,' I tell Louis. I will not weaken him.

'Huh?'

'You never make love to me.'

'What do you mean? We have loads of sex.'

'I know.'

Cassie

You two teddies sit together, squashed together. Smash, smash, smash each other, for your tea. I'll get you something to eat later. Don't move, be a good teddy baby now and behave. The baby gets smashed hard and it's ears are hard. It bites the back of my arm. Now my head is stiff and smacking happens. He cries, the baby, boo hoo hoo. No Uncle Toby, stay in the kitchen. Run teddy, run and hide behind Andi. But Andi's gone out. Where to now baby Teddy? Big Baby, Stupid Baby, Poor Baby. Run to Mammy, up the steps,

'Mammy, Mammy? Let Baby Teddy in. He has to get under your bed before Blackie buries him in the garden.'

I am Blackie. On all fours. I am the big black dog. I leave Mammy's door and turn around and jump on The Monster and bite his head off and throw it down the stairs. I did it, I saved Baby Teddy. The Monster is sulking downstairs and Blackie is happy. He goes in doing his doggy walk to Mammy's side and licks her. Be quiet Blackie, good dog, don't wake her. Is she pretend sleepy? I do that too. But I am better than her at it. She feels soft. If I get in on your side, Mammy, I can lick your face too. I won't wake you, in real life. Very gentle lick. I slide down where the duvet is hot and cosy, hide my head, so no-one will see me in here smiling.

Cally

Morning now and the sound of quietness in our still house.
I can hear everyone else busy outside. Dull thuds of lorries
thumping on the speed ramps, the roar of traffic made quiet
and I wonder how that is? Clattery voices merging into one
in the distance, the school bell silencing them and a few
out now doing PE and sounding distinct. That's making
it yellow out there and blue or pink in here. Downstairs
has that starting-to-go feeling I want to avoid, it's the only
time I can hear the fridge and next door coughing in their
kitchen with their radio on mumble. Head and foot cold
from poking out of the bed covers. Who will get up first to
make the tea? Whoever most needs to clear their crackly
stiff chest with a deep soothing breath of smoke. Waiting
for someone else to be first, to take responsibility when it's
too early and I'm too tired. Sometimes I can make my head
take a really big jump and skip that bit and get straight up.

It's the waiting for that which hurts, not the start itself. But I just can't do it today. Not yet. Not into the cold air. It's too sharp and I'm too fuzzy to be cut through. I lie listening to others doing it, long way away, for a bit longer. But I keep extending, alternating, justifying, caving-in. Always caving-in. Finally the lure of a mid-day sleep when they are at school is enough to pull me out of nothing into everything and I lean over to check the phone. Straining open slitty eyes to see. Blinking stiff disappointment and the failure of all the other days when I see its 9.30 a.m. now. Deciding whether to rush and make up for lost time or to resign myself to it and give in. Too big a decision to make and too difficult to walk into the school and have to explain to starchy knickers with all perfect Prefect hair and make-up done by 7.30 a.m. So Cassie's late. Just pretend it's a sick day. Tell Cassie she is sick so she remembers to say that she was sick. Turn over and see that Louis is still here.

'Louis, it's half nine. You're late,' he should wake himself up. What am I, his mother? 'Louis,' what did he do before me? Lazy tosser, 'wake up. It's late Monday,' set your alarm like everyone else. Not my job.

I turn over to read the story of me before the library wants me back and charges twenty cent a day for forgetting. That I'm her, Calypso, as I walk on Ogygia where the sea is clear at the bottom of mountains of olives. I escape here, in the mornings, because it's better than here, with Louis. I cavort with Gods of the Aegean. My Odysseus washes up on my beaches, all ship-wrecked and ransacked and smoking. I tempt him, I ride him, I hide him, making love nests in order to cover him. To keep him for myself for seven short years of bliss until, that is, his ex gets wind of it and gets bigger gods involved. They don't write stories like that anymore.

Louis

'What's Cassie doing in our bed? Hey you, get up for school. Your Mum forgot to get you up. Forgot to put you to bed more like, hey? Did you hide my alarm clock?'

'No, Blackie did,' says Cassie.

'So you dug a hole in the garden, put it in, and covered it up with mud. Why?'

'It was making Mammy cross.'

'Too right it was you tiny JCB. Tickly under there. Get away with you now. Hep. Hep. Get up. And get me that alarm clock,' blank speed. Singing, 'Angel of the Morning,' just good to be alive. And away downstairs, 'Angel of the Morning,' tea, smoke, sit. Sleep-full waking, a black and white test card left playing with the supermarket music trickling out of it and running down my ears. Don't have to know about, care about, The Big Questions. WTF? It's not like I have conversations with myself. That would be mad.

Pause, feeling like a specimen, Angel in the Morning gluing me to the page. Cassie is waiting for the open fridge to offer up the milk which is never there. I never feel there, but I'm in the mirror somewhere. Her security in having me, or anyone, tying her to the room. If there's a noise coming out of it, then that's enough for her to register belonging. Singing, humming, tapping musical notes to tell her I'm in. But they fill my head instead, take up all the space so there's no RAM left for anything else. Large music files. Sounds good. So I do it again. And again and I do it so much it happens on auto, a muffler for shutting-out the real noise. I can't control it, can't control the control. Now the real noise can't get in at all, even when I hear it screeching. When the ears aren't dripping with a life full of it.

Cassie gives up. On fridge or me? Can't hear her voice. She should get one. Who should do that? Get the voice to get the milk that Jack built? We roll around each other, connected and stuck here, no-one to pull us out of orbit. So we press our heads in further and carry on rolling.

Cassie

I spend all day not going to school. It is the best day ever. I have a teeny tiny family living in the corners of the skirting board. They're not mice, but they are about that size. They have an invisible house with four rooms in it, one for each of them. But they don't always stay in their own room. Sometimes, when I make a really nice room, they all want to live in it. There are lots of houses to choose from, going all around the kitchen floor. The postman goes to each one every day, even the old ones, and the daddy tells him to feck off with his bills. Today's house is number twenteen. It is really good and clean and nice and stuff and they have just moved into it because yesterday's house at number sixty-two was yucky and needed new carpets because some of them got melted. But it has a really nice mantelpiece with a white fireplace under it that makes the house warm without anyone lighting it. I'll move that into the new house. It's taking ages because there are two foxes in the front garden at number twenteen. They took over the trampoline and I have to get Blackie to scare them off. They keel over in fright and die. I put the two children on the trampoline and they bounce so high they can see across the whole wide world. Blackie buries the foxes under the grass. Andi once asked me why is there only one family living in the whole village? A 'diorama drama,' she called it. I told her one is enough. They get married, have children, grow up, get married and have more children, all of the time. They don't need anyone else.

I listen to the morning telly while I'm playing pretend houses. It has finished and now it's afternoon telly, repeats of everything that was on in the morning. I like that. They should repeat it in the morning too, then my game would be a bit quicker because the mammy can only get up after Ballamory has been on twice. There is a pink castle in Ballamory. My one is built behind the door. It is a very tall place for the very bad people. Sometimes it is very busy. And they come out all pink and nice again because the inventor living inside of it has made a special machine which does everything I want it to do to people. Like a car wash. I like playing with water in the sink too. It floods a bit. I slide around until it dries. Now I will be Blackie and go outside to play on the green with all the other children back from school. I walk around them first, sniffing. They run. I chase. I catch. And it's their turn and we're all running and screaming and laughing and falling and cold grass and liking I'm puffed out so muchness for ages and ages until I smell the air getting darker and some mammies start calling their kids in, one-by-one. We keep running to stay out for longer, run until it hurts, but still they keep on leaving to go inside. I am the only one left. Car lights shine over me and I watch them turn to park and leave me in the dark. Nine of them, I think. I'm nobody's business, my mammy always says.

So I go home.

Louis

It's unusual for me to be late for work. I'm a morning person, not normally a problem getting up for the commute. Music, driving, smoking, sitting back in the car. Just relaxing with, or without, the traffic jams. Driving over the Strawberry Beds and remembering growing up in Phibsborough's wildernesses down by the Royal Canal and the old freight lines. We started our own band down there by banging on the rusted oil drums. There was no one to hear us or to complain as we competed for airspace with Thin Lizzy and we roared like cowboys and indians. Then we'd lay railroad tracks in the prairie, getting lost for days at a time, as we built up our speed for running through the playing fields where Uncle Brown worked as a groundsman and we dared each other to knock on his hut. And he'd chase us out of it, apart from the ones he'd knock-on himself. I got so fast racing ahead of him they called me Zeus, from the Wonderwoman comic. Should've been Asterix. None of them fast enough. The thrill of it all and back in time for tea. Where the rake of us were packed into that tiny terraced house for spuds and boiled ham until Nan died and we knocked through to her house next door. Only after the coffin was gone, mind you. Everything left the same as when she was alive except for a doorway at the bottom of the stairs where we frayed her old-lady wallpaper passing between the houses. We were too afraid of her to change anything when us boys moved into all her old rooms, my bed alongside her glass cabinet, terrifying me still lest I break something in my sleep and she clips me one from the grave. The smell of moth balls and the African Violet sweets that she kept in her cardigan pockets to hand out to babbies when she worked the stalls down Moore Street. Then when she was getting on and no longer able for it we would be sent down town to her old market of a Saturday to do her shopping. And perish the child that didn't get it right, we'd be sent straight back if we didn't have the half pound of mince that could be bought only from Mackens, she knew if it wasn't, and the cabbage from Annie's which had a firmer heart than any you'd find in a corner shop. You couldn't get one past our Nan. She was a pro when it came to making you do things her way. Took bloody ages it did. Now it's all click and collect or staying in for a Tesco home delivery. That's how our business survived, how I've been in the trade for so long, by adapting, by keeping up with what the customer wants. Technology. There is always a way of fixing it, or of making it better if you just keep at it. That's what I tell the lads at work with their IT degrees and electrical engineering and can't even change a plug without unionising it and looking up their job descriptions. It's not rocket science I tell them, you are service technicians and I show them how to do what three years of college couldn't.

'You are Legend' they tell me, and I am.

So anyway it surprised them when I walked into the parts department late, at 10.30 a.m. Not right. Something amiss with the old reliable.

'Ah here, I had a dentist's appointment, cracking dental nurse,' good excuse, believable too, 'you not started yet? Toby in? He was at ours last night,' kipping somewhere. I escape into my office, my desk, KPIs to go through after checking the call-outs. I am busy on the phone when Murphy comes in. A walrus of a man whose blubber oozes sweat, a paean of success. Maybe I should eat more so I at least look like I want his job. Ex GAA, his once strapping body has loosened with age and the flattering beers bought by reverential fans with long memories. Some trade-off, as he slithers around the door-frame, wiping away his trail.

'Ah there you are Louis. I've been waiting for you. Free to talk?'

You're coming in anyway, not like I have a say in it. Don't yawn.

'What's the problem?' yawn. No problems here. Everything hunky-dory-malabory, 'not like you to come into the underworld of Parts and The Land That Time

Forgot. Grab a seat.'

'Louis. Just shut the door there. It's, it's, well it's like this. Awkward,' he starts.

Spit it out man. You're getting divorced. Your son's gay. Why you telling me?

'You see Louis, changes from the top.'

His fingers are together. Never good when the fingers meet. Or, he's leaving and I'm getting promotion.

'They thought you should know, well you would know, but I was requested to ask, well, to tell you,' sneaking a look up at me. I don't have a clue, 'it's just that, as it's been reported, have to be seen to act and all that. One of the girls might have seen something inappropriate on your computer.'

'What's inappropriate? Who was it? What was she even doing in here?'

'No, no, she wasn't snooping. In passing. Just saw. Just saying. You do know what I'm talking about don't you Louis? Good, good, I knew you were good. Embarrassing. So…we'll leave it at that shall we? Say no more. Best not discuss it with anyone. Jobs worth and all that. Well best be on. Ah uh difficult one. So, to be clear, we're good to go, yes?' tapping his nose.

Because? Christ,

'Yes. Yes of course,' Jesus wet. Say he's right. Is that the right answer? What just happened? Say no more? 'bye then,' confused raised eyebrows to let the sense in. Of what? The lads are staring at me oddly through the glass. They know.

Know what?

'Feck it lads, what was all that about? Murphy came in, said a load of nothing in no seconds flat and disappeared. What am I meant to "know already"?'

They are all looking at each other.

'Huh? Tell me.'

And then more actual head-widening confusion. Toby had been sacked as soon as he'd got into work. Hauled into HR and came out black, got his gear and ordered off the premises. Not even a leaving party. Gardening leave? Redundancy? No warning, nothing, and no explanation. I thought I was getting it too there. As if. It's too expensive to let me go. I must have been here thirty odd years. Thirty, and trying to think of them. Not one year comes to mind. They can't afford to make me redundant. A good wedge for Toby though. Wonder how much he got? Enough for a house, or a car, or to buy me one? Which of the lads will they pick to go too? Do they think Boss was asking me to pick them out? 'I wasn't, you know, discussing any of you', I didn't know he was talking redundancy, 'rabbiting he was,' they saw the nose-tapping. Oh crap, they think I'm in on it. Pick, pick pick at the scaly itchy hands. Poor Toby. Thought he was out on a call. Who's going to cover for him? Red, scratch and pus. Bewildered but panicky too. Stomach reacting to all this stuff. Run to the loo. Ah the relief as my bowels drain out of my head, down into the bowl and away. As good as a nicotine blanket. Soothe and gently close that box.

Now back to dealing with the day. Work mode box open. The efficiency of it. Functions and sliding, gliding, from task to task. Easing in, and easing out. Getting it done and getting more done and time passing and going through the motions blindfolded. It's an ease to please each customer on the phone and service contracts racking up the figures way past targets. Way past fast. The stress of it. And now it's gone half past five. Surprise that the service department is empty. Toby is usually here waiting for a going-home-fag and what-are-your-travails. Straining to comprehend how the work-sheet that never ends tells a different story, very few jobs were done today. Staring at lint sticking to healed sores in hope of inspiration. Not finding the thing that happened today. Grabbing at grabbing but nothing there. Holding breath but still it's just an empty furlong of memory. Another omission. Not shared. I give up. Instead I ease myself, please myself into the security of the familiarity of an empty office, and the thrill that it just might not be. I log off the client account and by-pass the basic security designed by me to stop me from doing exactly what I'm doing right now.

I open the web cam which covers our home security system, streaming live at the moment. I installed it myself to ensure maximum coverage so no-one can break in without us knowing and so it will capture video of the burglar. That's how I explained it to Cally. Made up, she was, that I was so concerned about her. It made her feel safe and loved and all. Easiest thing in the world to watch her in bed.

Dimness of the cowness. She swears blind she has never fantasised but we've seen her do it too many times to bother with all the video files. Just look at this week's version. Not bad at all. She could be doing it in her sleep. Like she wants that burglar to walk in now and rape her. I load that one and log into my file-sharing account to see what the others have put up today. Nice stuff from MIKE1270 in the more specialist section. It's all about the photography, I'm interested in the artistic and technical side of things. Such as contrast and shade, composition and the difficulty of maintaining focus. They have to like what they're doing in order to do what they're doing. Toby is in my head and I'm kneeling and skirted. I log out and uninstall, backtracking though all my footprints. Virgin snow. Waste, I know.

Andi

I skive off double PE to avoid the warm-ups and all that pretending to be stupidly fit when all we really do is lounge about the sports hall while the basketball players show us how good they are and we never get a turn because we're crap at it. We're just lining the walls, invisible in our ugly tracksuits. A necessary foil to reflect the stars that shine. Rather that than bounce my double GGs. It's easy to sneak out when the teacher is engaged and isn't looking because he's got his fiancée and can concentrate on teaching. Not like some of the pervs, who perv on pervs. Easy to slide away on my own without a slidey eye following you round the room. No one joins me today. That's not to say I'm a loner or anything. I don't get picked on. I keep my head down, don't stand out, I don't want to, I just get by. So that's why, when I go, no one knows I'm missing. I go for a smoke along the towpath. It should be quiet down here now all the 'auld ones are in their book clubs or shopping down at B&Q. Someone is heading towards me though and I chuck my lit fag in the canal so I can ask him for a light.

'You're too young to be smoking,' he says.

'Are you going to give me one or not?'

He smiles as he takes his lighter out, his dog wagging around my legs.

'Don't you know dog-walking time is over?' I ask him.

'Don't you know play-time is over?'

'Fair enough. You going to tell?'

He takes his phone out, the bastard. But instead of ratting he does a selfie of us 'as evidence' and says, smiling, that he needs my number to Snapchat it to me. Not grassing then.

'Let you off if you go back into school,' he says as if it's his job to make me. But I want him to make me, 'stay in touch,' waving his phone at me as I do as he tells me.

I watch us getting fit from the side-lines.

Cally

I just get to the good bit where Perseus is running across the Adriatic with that snakey head of Medusa. Still looking, I bet she is, trying to get a gawk up his skirt before he turns invisible, when the phone rings. Chains dangling. It's Toby. Says he's been made redundant and can't I put in a good word for him, as if I could, and when I can get a word in I don't know what to say. What's appropriate? Isn't there a way out? What should I think? He frets, not like him. A lot, like he's the only one in the world bad things happen to. The Ancients.

'Really Toby, I'm so sorry. What'll you do?' and what about Louis, it dawns on me, was he let go too? My throat's too tight. Everything's suddenly tangled up, being blown down the street and out into the desert. All our futures tumbling at high speed in slow motion, over and over again, into impossible and desperate scenarios. Neighbours staring at my back. My insides lurch. No they don't. That's horse-riding isn't it, or is it lunge? Lurching and lunging into the charred remains. It's the shock of it. Speak, 'but why? Are they down-sizing, being taken-over? Louis never said anything to me,' glad it's you and not Louis. Neither of you would get a job. Celtic Tiger boom, bust and back again but you're too old, 'are you coming back here?' please don't not with that misery head on you. Downer. The pair of you. I've enough going on. Oh God give me strength. Or Xanax, 'you must come and have dinner,' Andi can get in a take away. Stuff happening to my head. Get off the phone will you. Head shouting, 'you'll be okay Toby. We're here for you. You know that don't you? You can always stay here,' always flipping do anyway, 'you know you're always welcome,' buy your own bleeding house. Divorced, jobless, loser. He'd live on your ear, that one. The cost of it, 'Louis' brother is my brother, you know that,' just grow up will you? Loud temples and shouty teeth. Growling throat stays silent. He's not talking at all now. He's being such hard work. If he'd just get off the phone, 'I can hear Louis' car now. See how he is. Talk later. Bye. Bye,' with that moustache and quiff I'd sack Toby too. Seventies' throwback. Louis too, with the big shiny suits. They are way too big for him, jacket almost down to his knees. It doesn't make him look taller, he shrinks inside of them.

'Hi Louis. What's up at work today, Toby get sacked? Just been onto him,' what happened, will you be made redundant too? Less money for us or a big cheque? What about after that? I have to be nice, 'you're tired,' pulling the weariness out of the bridge of your nose. How I hate that mark where your glasses were digging into your head. Get some that fit. Get a suit that fits. God, you always think that you're bigger than you are. Wasn't your mother great? You're not so confident now, hey? They might be getting rid of you at work. Then you'll know how I feel. Get a job, get a job. Can I have two euro, beg, beg, grovel. Prick.

'No. Not me.'

The relief when you say that. And the doubt, 'odd, don't you think, that they only made one person redundant? Is it going to be a long, drawn out, tortuous dismissal thing? Picking you off one by one. They should just tell you all in one go. It's not fair to leave us all guessing and worrying. Poor Toby. I told him, I did, what a shame for him. A man his age. How's he going to get another job at his age? On gardening leave until the redundancy kicks in? At least he'll get paid for doing nothing for a while. May get used to that,' that's mean, 'not that he wants to get used to it. He'll just have to. Not helping, sorry. You must be so worried about your job, about Toby. Terrible.'

I play the worried wife part. But I am worried, about how much I'm supposed to say. I keep quiet. Was it about both you and Toby? I lock it in and concentrate. Your misery is more cheering than mine. I mustn't let you see me smile at that though. Glide you into the kitchen and smooth your ills away. Beers tonight. Cheers tonight. Any excuse night. For you and me, avoid the fury. Expert that I am. That I should be. In fact I shouldn't be. Drawn into this dance around your reactions. A life of dodging, of covering up, of avoidance and of making way for you. All the clues I had when we were young, to step away from this relationship, to make another choice. Then sticking to the comfort of sticking to what I was comfortable with. Our second date when we partied with Toby's friends and you were paralytic drunk. But it wasn't just that, it was the vicious way you spoke to me, full of bile and hate and you explained it away the next day as a drinking binge, a blur, an aberration, it would never happen again just give it another chance, you said, you weren't like that at all. Nah, really? Shucks you were such a nice guy. I wanted more of that. It must have been me, if you said so, keeping you out late. Training me in, reining me in, and shaping my ebb and flow. When you proposed, simmering and shouting at my friends all evening, thinking that would get rid of them. It did. I didn't say no. Then turning on me at the bar, angrily demanding I marry you. What better place to begin? It was a threat, not an offer of love and I had to oblige, I couldn't say no. And my 'yes' caught you out. It was retaliation, a hollow triumph for me. Did you mean to continue, to be mean? Then the embarrassment when I insisted on it the next day, when you couldn't even remember it or take it back like everything else. You too weak to say you didn't really mean it. Me too weak to let it go. No wonder Toby was in such a bad mood on our wedding day. At the accidental promise. At revenge's revenge. He knew we were meant for each other. But he was jealous that I was taking you away from him. Two little boys had two little toys, still fighting the urge to creep back into bed with each other. His whipping post gone, you tying me to mine. Just move on down the line. It's too exhausting to think about. Beer or wine? If I open a bottle you will drink it all before I get a chance, then you'll have all of the beer too. Calculating that at least you'll black out quicker and I won't need to acquiesce to your violent silent needs, while I silently say 'no.'

Louis

Cally's hovering. Like a vulture picking over me. Revelling in it. Back off woman. Just leave me be. All my worries, the weight of it all. She has no idea, just swans about making everyone's life a misery with her nosey nagging scraggy neck. And those nostrils, a pig could live in them. Relentless, she is. What's the bet she's going straight to the fridge now, look at her, taking my beer out and deciding it's her wine, controlling me while helping herself. Greedy bitch if she thinks she's having it. I paid for all that. I'm only in the door and she's winding me up in my own home when all I want is to wind down. Just leave me alone and stop pecking at me.

She is offended by my shiny suit. It carries her resentment. Seventeen years' worth. I remove the jacket and feel bigger without it. She notices and lightens, maybe, something like that? She likes my heat, comes close.

Flitting around me, she touches my face and says things will be alright. She likes it when I'm angry. I tap it out for her and the dance of hormones begins. She is my lover, she cannot resist the sparking and the silently remarking it's highly charged in here isn't it? The danger of the danger as she refuses to accept she is the problem in the room. She dances around all that. Temptress wrapped in an old nag's skin. She pulls back, feigns survival. She's on thin ice, all this backwards and forwarding. I know she is cajoling me into a false sense of life, is so terribly nice. She thinks she'll be safe if we drink ourselves stupid and she offers me night-time treats with a suggestive wink and a twinkle and I'll be up for you in a minute dear just let me make you a nice hot whiskey before I finish you off. And hopefully she will, before she has to. She doesn't always deliver on time. Then to make her aware of her scheming, for her getting it wrong, I've got to be strong. Because it could end up anywhere if I'm not willing to give her a good kicking in the legs where no one will see her idiocy. She must have fallen down the stairs she'll say obediently, but too late. It wasn't me, you see. She just keeps on falling, stupidly. It's true. Admit nothing.

I slump back into my spot, she shrunk me again, waiting for a night full of things which will never happen. I've bigger worries to think about. Toby, and what about me? Final wages, fall in status, fraying suits? If I were to lose my job too? But Toby was careless. He should have known better. No wonder they're keeping it quiet at work. Couldn't have a scandal, losing business and a momentary handle on his moment of discovery. They shouldn't have been looking. At least you can rely on their discretion. And that's what really worries me, just how much can I rely on other people's discretion, on secrets and lies, on them keeping things buried at work until they've died? I worry that Cally will dig, dig, dig away at me until she finds the real reason why Toby was let go. She just doesn't know when to stop that woman. Evil, she is. It makes me mad again that she will go on and on about redundancy, picking away until she's got it out of me, until she knows. I hate her for it. Me and Toby, now, we know when to talk and when not to. It's a skill. She doesn't have it. The whole stinking lot of her is building up inside of me, on top of today. My gut is pushing against it. I throw it all up, shock and vomit showers over the kitchen table. Gross out. Everyone is running in to see and running around caterwauling. Women and their panics.

'It's just a tummy bug,' I tell them. Obvious.

Cally lifts everything up and away in the tablecloth. It disappears as though nothing occurred. She knows well to keep her thoughts to herself at these times. Cassie looks appalled and fascinated, inspecting the floor for carrot in the remains of sick and hiding some under the press. My stomach torments me after, rather than before, the event. Typical. I try squeezing the pain out. Jeeez it's hard enough to get any sympathy in this house.

'I've not eaten for twelve hours. It must be dead by now?' I plead. Anyone?

'When you have secrets they leave a gap in you,' Cassie states.

'You mean they fill you up, with guilt,' I correct her.

'No. A gap. Where it hurts. Like a hungry tummy does,' she explains.

'So what do you eat for that?'

'Children.'

'For feck's sake, only cannibals do that.'

'Even cannibals wouldn't, well, apart from the Egyptian ones,' Cally joins in, more concerned about their kids than me.

'I don't think Daddy's going to eat me,' quite right Cassie, 'maybe Andi,' she adds.

'What? No. I'm just saying, that's all.'

'But your tummy hurts so you will have to eat a baby,' Cassie insists.

'I have a gap because I haven't eaten all day. I am not full of secrets and I do not eat babies.'

'Not "full of secrets". She means you have gaps left by secrets,' Andi corrects me.

'How can a secret leave a gap? Secrets fill you up till they burst out of you.'

'Like your sick,' observes Cassie.

Gross.

Andi

I hang around the kitchen. Mum looks awkward. It nearly turns into one of those parent-daughter I've got to talk to you but only because you are standing there moments. Of course she's got nothing to say, so buggers off to hide again. Until life is over and she can come out to play. Someone should tell her. Cassie isn't here either. No one notices. Every night.

'Either eat something, or stop worrying the fridge,' Dad quips.

He saw me shutting the doors, three times each. He says I do it on purpose to annoy him. I do it on purpose because it annoys me if I don't.

'Just eat something. Anything at all. Look at you. A stick insect. A puff of wind could blow you away. And then you'd be stuck, floating around in the sky,' he sneers, pleased with this.

I won't eat, not after his sick. But still he pulls me into our world of friendly hate. It's called family love. If I step into it I'll never step out. Bit of taunting, pressing old buttons, bitching backwards and forwards and digging and flicking when all he has to do is let go but no-one's told him how to cut it with an interval. My brain shrivels. In with a plan, Dad gets drunk, gets easy, I get in there before he gets nasty.

'Dad. You're really white. Have some water,' butter him up, 'what with that and Uncle Toby today.'

'What do you want?'

That was blunt. Maybe I was too obvious.

'Nothing. You've just been sick. Just worried that's all,' play it slow. Maybe too soon. Slip it in under the conversation to allow it to work. It just takes a little time to manoeuvre him into position, then pang, into the wallet. Ho hum. Wipe down the table. Get him another beer. Appear useful. Swing the duster around for a bit, 'but there is one thing...'

'Ah here we go. I knew it. What? I don't have it, whatever it is.'

'It's just that I'm on the basketball team next week,' breaking his shite laughing he is now. That's the way to do it, gets him every time, 'so I'll be needing forty euro,' and that's double what I need and he'll end up giving me...twenty, 'cheers Dad. Thanks,' how easy was that? It could've gone either way. Can I get any more while I'm at it? While he's sad he isn't angry. Cheer and flirt, it's as easy as that. Big smile. Easy cheesy. Leave the hand out for five seconds more...lemon squeezy...raise the eyebrows so I'm not really asking so he can't blame me for anything...and yes! His hand is going back to the wallet and out comes... wait for it...get up close...I'd sit on his lap but that's too obvious...wow a fifty, just tell him it's a, 'tenner, thanks Dad,' yep, too pissed to even notice. Poor old Dad. Aw isn't he cute when he's tired like that? Want to squidge him. My elbows press into my ribs instead. Invisible-hug-me's. Smiles are pushing out from the inside, squashing my eyes. If he tells me to do anything in return I would right now. I wouldn't back-out or go get some credit, ask if he needs anything at the shop and then resent him because he'll tell me to buy it out of the money he just gave me. No, I'd buy it for him and not stay out so long that he forgets ever asking me to get anything. If he wants to drink it's because he needs to. He doesn't drink often, only at the weekends, obviously, and on a Thursday night because it's nearly the week-end. Then on a Monday because it's such a long way until the week-end, you gotta have something to cheer the week up. And on a Wednesday because it's the middle of the week. And on Tuesdays because of the football or he wants to watch a film so you may as well have a few crisps and a beer to make a movie night of it, 'have a brandy,' I offer, 'that's good for a sore tummy. Mum hides a bottle in with the cooking stuff. There you go,' not even a calculated move. I'm not even trying to knock him out quick. I'm just being helpful and getting Cassie ready for bed and I won't go out, wait for him to pass out, avoid the gropes, sneak the heating on, send texts from a bath that's way too hot when he's fast asleep and he can't give out to me about immersions. I don't need to keep on thinking any of that. Got my own life instead, in the real world. Chat to my own friends on Facebook, Snapchat, whatever. Here's a fairly new one. He has a nice profile so I accepted him the other day. It's going good. Know him well now.

Him:	sup
Me:	head office giv me 20 + 50 euro
Him:	deadly credit
Me:	easy money ☺
Him:	;)
Me:	back atcha
Him:	hve sex wit me
Me:	as in foto
Him:	fk yeah
Me:	cd9 bath ltr
Him:	txt foto
Me:	I got it frst time
Him:	2b sure u kno i want u
Me:	☺
Him:	open mouth
Me:	what EMOJI is that
Him:	2 rude. Its got a wide mouth :O
Me:	lol u that big
Him:	only 4 u

Me: shw me ltr
Him: show me too

Maybe I will. Show me how not to. Guess I'll have to. Want to anyway. Do ya, don't ya, do ya, don't ya, do ya, don't ya? Do it in the bath. With bad hair. How's that gonna work? Getting back in after it's all washed and dried and it's freezing and frizzy, and crap. Or back in my room with just fairy lights on so he can't really see me? Hide the teddies and move the posters to hide the stupid babyfying wallpaper that I loved so much when she got it for me. So stupid. And Mum upstairs all this time hiding from Dad. It should be her down here standing between me and him, not the other way around. He's mostly okay. You just got to read him right, know when to disappear. She can't time it, gets it wrong on purpose. Wrinkled belly and massive toes. Such noise when she swallows her tea. It'll gross you out just being in the same room as her. I wish they could just… growling angry explosions ripping the back of my head off. Instead I pull one hair out at a time, letting little bits of fury out until one day I'll be bald but my head'll be empty and my parents won't be chewing my brain. One day, what, how will it be different? She says this, he says 'crap', they wind each other up, shout, bawl, hide, hate, and kiss and make up and on and on it goes forever more. Taking ages to die that way and while she takes a swipe at him what she's really doing is taking a swipe at me, digging into me. Four times and the fryer turns on. Try being nice to each other, it'll be

62

nice for me. Hello, I do exist in here you know. That radio noise when you've stopped listening. Turn it off and then you notice. Exclamation mark. The relief. If I stood in the fridge would he notice? Or if I curled up in the saucepan, no too dirty, or if I was suspended. The world's tidiest teenager hanging upside down under the table. Not quite dropping, but nearly, and waiting to be found, holding in a squeal then letting it out anyway. Dead giveaway. I go upstairs.

Me:	in my room get reddy 4 me
Him:	always reddy
Me:	how so
Him:	sendng pic. reddy?
Me:	big pic. yea reddy
Him:	what bout u?

I don't know, so don't reply. No means no so why not just say it? He won't hang about.

Him:	I'm still reddy n waiting 4 u 2 show me too

I still don't know what to do, so do nothing.

Him:	let me tell you bra off and take foto. press send. happy me

Like that's how you text. Just do it. Leave my head out, that way he can't prove it's me, pose with shoulders back, hold breath, pull everything in, turn side-on so they're bigger, no I'll try the front view from below, press and send. One, two, three, four seconds. He should have it by now. Why hasn't he replied? Are they too small or too big? Normal? Maybe another one but press them together to make them seem huge. Phone up high, pointing down at them. Press and send.

Wait...Still no reply. What's wrong with them? I'll hold them both up with one arm, press and send. Waiting still. What else should I do? Keep trying until he likes one of them. Press and send. Maybe it's too dark, turning all the lights on so he can see them properly. Press and send. Close up and send. Would you come on and appreciate my effort.

Me: dnt u like them
Him: this is how much i like them

I open the video clip. Wow. I did not know that, exactly. Well I did, just not seen anyone do it. Want to see anyway. Push my mouth to one side.

Me: nice
Him: how nice? Show me
Me: wot a video
Him: yea a vid
Me: ok

No bloody way. Of what? You have got to be kidding.

How do you do that? Can't let him know I've no idea how to do it and look right, and avoid the embarrassing wallpaper and get the right light and hold the phone and push my boobs up all at same time. Impossible.

Me: but i cant hold fone and do it at same time
Him: cool do it anyway and send a vid

Oh man. Do what?

Me: wot u want me to do
Him: grate i tel u.............

And that's how it starts and I get good at following instructions and at lighting and at camera shots and at all sorts of weird shit angles that have nothing to do with me fancying him but with him fancying me if I do it right. I know exactly what I will do to him when we meet in real life and then I get to show him off as the best-looking lad they've ever seen. Well fit, he is. He wants to meet me too and do all that, but I said we'll just meet first. He's asked his mate to drive him down to my school at lunch break Wednesday, says their school has the afternoon off, so we can go down the canal and shift a bit under the bridge, pretend we're smoking.

Me: cant wait to meet u

I reckon I've got nothing to lose now he's seen everything.

Him:	u wont regret it i promis
Me:	we can go to ur hse after
Him:	no can do babes
Me:	where do u live
Him:	guess
Me:	in town?
Him:	closer 2u
Me:	in my village?
Him:	closer
Me:	how so?
Him:	guess
Me:	i cant but i wud hav seen u
Him:	u hav
Me:	huh?
Him:	i went past u yesterday
Me:	u never did
Him:	in my frends car
Me:	wot car he got?
Him:	blue mazda
Me:	same car as my uncle u kno him?
Him:	we know him so
Me:	u lik him?
Him:	i dont fancy him lol
Me:	gross
Him:	not lik u. ur lovely grate pics n vids

Me: u like?

Him: cudnt c ur face tho shame want 2cu all

Me: wuz holding fone in my mouth

Him: thinking it wuz me

Me: of corse

Him: splendid

Me: splendid? What kinda jerk r u?

Him: a splendid one wot u want to jerk off lol lol

Me: u kno me so wel

Him: kno u better wensday cant wait

Me: me too. So whos this mate with the car same as my uncles?

Him: mazda man?

Me: mazing

Him: mite let us use the car

Me: front or back?

Him: u wicked getting me hot

Me: not like that tho i cud if u want

Him: i want

I don't.

Me: i do 2

Him: b4 wensday or i wil die

I won't.

Me: me 2

Little puff of happy on the inside comes up and out and I lie awake thinking of all the things we will do when we're pressing up hard against each other and thinking of all the things that I really won't do but have said that I will and how to get around that when we really meet and he really does want to do it. Maybe put him off until next week when I'll feel more like it. When I'll feel like more of a feel, instead of pretend and play. Alright, he's just pretending too. Wouldn't know what to do. Scared lads can't say it any more than we can. Doesn't stop the homing devices in their fingers and dicks. Timid pigeons always finding their way. Nesting in bras. So how did anyone meet before the internet? No wonder parents hate each other. Never tried each other out.

Listening to them getting at each other downstairs. Why does that bug me and make Cassie so nervy? When they start she does that running on tippy-toes thing. They think it's cute but it's not, because she's pretending not to be there by barely touching the floor. Or she's Blackie the dog either burying their hate in a hole in the garden or trying to be cuter than herself. People get pets when they can't love their kids properly. I don't think my parents like dogs either. Or sky dancers.

It's gone quiet now so I guess Cassie must be in bed, so I can go down and watch TV battle-free. Mum won't reappear. Dad's hugging the table. I get just five minutes of it when the doorbell rings and I'd bet my sister on it that no-one will answer, they'll ring again, then knock in case the bell's broken and knock again louder this time in case we didn't hear the first time which of course we all did and we're all just waiting for me to get up and see who it is.

'I'm not paying sponsorship,' Dad shouts, loud enough for them to hear.

Mum isn't in, even though she is. Cassie hasn't woken otherwise she'd be driving me mental by now to open the door. She really is like a dog then. I'll go see the perfect lad waiting, wondering to himself why he never saw how amazing I am and I'll be standing there, haloed in the hall light and he'll be stunned into silence and awed by my flowing wit. Until he sees the zit. So no, I won't answer. Dad gets a text. Put it on silent, duh, and goes to the door himself. Toby's voice pours through the hall before he does. Hear carrier bags of cans. A night full of commiserations. They come into the living room to deliberately ruin my space by filling it. They can't talk at a normal level, have to shout for Dad or have to shout for being men. Dad copies Toby at being a man, strutting around the place whenever he remembers. They can't even sit down without attacking the sofa with their weight in case someone might mistake them for little girly boys. Do they even know I'm here? They look like they are dancing together when they get up to swap seats and grab a hold of each other midway, anyone would think they were flirting. Then they revert to being macho, looking for a fight. They get drunk instead, which makes them worse, and they talk about the job or not having a job or getting a job and what job and what a great job it is not having a job. God they talk such boring shite. I've headphones on and they are hilarious in their silent movie of posturing, pouting and leaning-in to show each other themselves. Brotherly love, hey? And sharing the lurve now, spreading it around in my direction with his leery looks and greasy skin and silent grin. I stare straight ahead at the TV, don't risk engagement, but still have to sneak a look to be sure they are sure that I am sure that I don't want them to be here. And for no reason that slowly makes me angry and sideways I can see they are angry too and we are all angry and waiting for an excuse. And the waiting and the pretending makes it bigger until it fills the room and squashes us hard up against the walls, until Dad leans over and says something I can't hear but I see his drippy mouth move and smell his voice and know I don't like it when he hurts my arm and he laughs as his hand is up my leg too far and I snap now the little shite takes it away like I'm stupid for storming off upstairs in a hissy fit of bleedin' shaggin' hormones he probably says. Meteor shower.

Toby

Andi is watching TV with her headphones on, blocking us out, squashed up at one end of the sofa. Not yet a woman, not mouthy yet. Louis bounces between the two of us, excited. Moving constantly, jamming his stick-legs wide open, flapping his sketchy arms with tappy hands, tapping it into his tappy knees, tapping it into the floor like something real exciting is about to happen but you know that it won't. When he's had five beers this will stop, seven and he'll be almost comatose, won't finish eight. And then she will unfurl and let herself be there again. She thinks I can't see her when she does invisibility. I pretend that I can't, but I'm being complicit with her against the idiot in the middle. Still, I know she is there, hiding in full view. I protect her like she's my own daughter. Love, Uncle, strong. Animal ready to snap, punch and pummel into the ground anyone who comes near to harming my family. Even Louis,

71

I'd die for him. Watching-out for them all, here in the background. I've always had their backs, even in the back of the groundsman's hut. Me taking it like a man because they knew that I could and they only joined in if they wanted to, said our Uncle Brown. But the air was different in there as we pretended to kneel and pray but that's not what we were doing but that's what we did. Smelt of creosote and grass. We didn't have a choice and when we'd gone in once we knew we had to go in again, for our sins. Or something like that, I don't know, it's hard to explain. The pull and the pain. Why we went in to play the game? We were only kids, knocking about. Nothing much different from the alleys, just heavier, good practise. Sure, everyone did that. Helping my gang. Still here for them now at the head of the pack. You can't be listening to all these liberal whingers, bringing you down, like that Christine who took over as head of HR. That's when things started to go wrong. Another one telling me what to do, as if I'd take that. She wanted to be boss but didn't know how to do authority, that leadership thing, be a man with a dick. So she nagged passive-aggressively when what she really needed to do was to get laid, get a life and stop pretending in that tight skirt that all she wanted was a fuck and that would sort her out. Getting paid for giving me hard-ons. Paid a lot, it's criminal, the whore. And then there's my half-wit brother licking the ground she walks on as she crushes him into the pavement with her pointy stilettos as she stands on his back sliding her heel into his crack and he's pushing down on me, getting in there. In here. He watches me in that way and I need to beat that look out of him and give him one where he wants it.

TV ads come on showing holidays in the sun. Another one and no job to take a holiday from. Already had some job offers though. Might give them a go, after relaxing for a bit and revelling in the free-flow of sympathy. Enjoying a lie-in or two before going out there with a double-up wage and redundancy pay and nobody knows how much I have and I've a few more days to decide how much is enough to show off and how too much will attract the beggars asking for a hand-out. Shout and beat them back down, begging for mercy from old Uncle Brown. Bare-bottomed minors, licking the ground. I'm getting it anyway, getting away with it, doing the same, do as I say. So tell them I'm clearing divorce debts and that I've just enough left for a new car, man. Money in my hand and I'll have a new job soon, stop worrying and chill. Louis doesn't notice me spacing off in my mind but Andi could. She's sharp that one, like me. With her eagle-eyes, waiting, circling up in the silent air thermals. Another five years and she'll pause, calculate, spiral down to her target to pluck out its heart in one clean swoop. Then she'll scavenge, hacking away in torment on men's bodies, minds, their sanity. That's women for you. Soft on the outside, nasty on the inside. But right now she's on the edge of being like that, busy building up her resentments and scrawling them up into a wire ball that'll scratch away at her.

Louis

This is grand. I like this beer Toby got. Nice of him to bring it over. I'll be nice to him seeing as he lost his job today. He'll be alright getting another one. He's like that. And he's no mortgage or family to pay for anymore, so no big deal for him. It's not like he's got anything to lose. If it was me now, big problem. All this I've built up, down the swanny and starting all over again. Where to start? Who would get me a job now our Mam's dead? Like a goldfish swimming down the toilet bowl. Looking up I see one there on the sideboard. Sent to save me.

'I didn't know we had a fish Andi. When did we get that?' I ask her and have to give her a hard prod for not listening, 'Andi?'

'Ow. What Dad?'

That'll teach her.

'The fish?'

'What about it?' she almost says cretin.

'I said, when did you get the fish?'

She puts the 'phones back on to shut me out, to ignore my life. How ignorant.

'Cassie got that over a year ago and you only just noticed,' she lies, about me.

I'm only making conversation. I can't even talk now. Moody teenagers. What she sitting so far away for? You smell or something? Just be normal like me and Toby here before everyone notices and they start calling you a freak, 'everything okay at school?' I couldn't do with having a kid no one likes. She's still not listening. Come on, join in, little kitty mouse in the corner there. Cute and folded up into a ball with her soft hair falling. Ain't she the prettiest? And I made that. She's got me to thank for that, we're a good-looking family we are. She's got my genes so she's beautiful like me. Perfect, you are. Aren't you the best, like me? 'turn over to Sky Sports there,' I can talk about that. Toby thinks he can, shouts to win the conversation, but it's me who knows the most about football nowadays. She won't turn over the channel. Charm and disarm. And away she goes and I have parenting sorted. Easy. Look and learn Toby, look and learn. I've gotta ask why he's wearing that brooch, for God's sake.

'Toby. What's that white ribbon thing you got on there?'

'This huh? Stop violence against women. Hate that shit. Weakness, it is, not controlling yourself. You know, like, you're not a real man until you can stop yourself from hitting her lights out when she's a pain in the arse and really deserves a smack.'

'Haha.'

'Not funny, Louis, taking advantage of someone weaker than you. Cowardly. I disagree with it. Gotta man-up.'

'Yea, yea, I know. I agree. I'd never do that. Makes me mad thinking about it. It's terrible. But you do that all the time, to everyone. Why let women off?'

'Come on you're better than that.'

'In denial man.'

'You, or me?'

'You what?'

Exactly.'

Still what? Talk straight Toby. Sometimes I have absolutely no idea what you are saying, or really mean to be saying. You think too much and come out with all this crap that no-one understands, not even yourself, while sitting there all smug-faced like you won an argument which I wasn't even involved in. And there it is again, the condescending vibe. He tries my patience. I try to be nice and this is what I get back. Well I'll get my own back. There's stuff I know, and he knows I can use that if I want to. It's my secret too, but it's mine to give away as much as it's his to keep. Not saying I will. Just saying, that's all.

'Here Toby, have another drink,' to shut the hole. And fill the void, for the time being, or forever and a day. As long as you continue drinking to fill it nothing will come out. And the rest of us just blabber-mouths after a few jars, whores to our secrets and inner lives. And I'm in your story Toby, inside your head of histories, running around inside it and dangerously changing the endings. You're scared I'll remember everything, or scared I've forgotten. Perhaps it was different for me. We look at the same shared past but the camera angle back then was turned 180 degrees and we were stood side by side. So even then it was different, by a few paces. And we think we had the same childhood experiences, but we were planets away. There's my version and then there's yours. They were never the same, not even then. Life was happening to me, but you were the one always making it happen, writing the script. I went along with you, acting it out, because it was scarier not to. And you are still here operating me through fear, controlling what comes out of my mouth in case I incriminate you. In case I incriminate me. And neither of us is sure what it is anyway because we never spoke about it and never will and there's just this massive wall with the pressure of a hydro dam behind it and an army of self-preservation in front of it and I don't know what the hell it's about, so I ask him,

'Toby?'

'Yes.'

'Nothing,' as usual it can't come out of my mouth, it isn't big enough to eat the army and the dam all in one bite, 'just weary.'

'Don't. Don't go there,' he says, like he's bugged my mind. And he wipes clean the hard drive with a night of drinking to ease me into forgetting. Which I will.

Cassie

I watch a thin line of TV through the crack in the door. I hold my breath each time it tries to come out and count to three so no one will hear me. For forever, really. I can see. I hope they can't see me, so I hide at the side and slide along hall walls into the dark kitchen. I am an extra special secret agent sent to spy on my village in the skirting boards. While they are sleeping. But they are cheating. They are all awake and running around their housing estate at night-time. I didn't say you could wake up! I open the fridge and they are caught in the light. Stand still and pay attention, the loud speaker says. They are too scared to move. Sit down on that little sofa and let me tell you what I think of that. Wag, wag, wag. I take a beer off the table and give it to them. Pour it over their heads. They lean over, lean in, swim. Drinking and swimming and I tap them on the ground to dry. Just quiet little taps but it's hard really and it hurts and they cuddle each other instead of crying. Cuddle too much and one jumps up and throws herself across the kitchen. Bad girl. For making him do that. I will shut the fridge door for that. See how you like it. In the castle dungeon.

She sits in chains at the bottom of the dark hole. Looking up to the top, she can see stars twinkling and that's nice, she doesn't have to be scared if she can see them. Clouds move, she moves, around the edge of her pit. She keeps looking. For her stars.

Louis

I arrive in work. Something isn't right, again. I can't say what it is yet but there are signs. I can't say what the signs are yet either, but I'm picking up that feeling. A collection of differences that are setting off a warning. The light is different, or the sound. Strange vibe in reception as I walk through to my department. It's big, but I still can't see it. And there it is in my office, a large empty space where my computer was, there is nothing. But that isn't what's big, I know that. I know the fact that it is missing is smaller than the reason why it is missing. I am frozen in fear, weighted by all the fears of all the times I felt like this. And outcomes punch me at lightning speed. The overload makes it impossible to make any sense and I realise the pointlessness of trying. For a brief second calm settles but the onslaught quickly resumes. And so it continues. Years of this yo-yoing pass by in thirty seconds. Instinctively I sit to call Toby for help. Then I notice my desk phone has gone too. Hidden by Cassie? 'No it was Blackie,' she'd say. Relief as I realise it could only be redundancy. I sit and wait with head laid out on the table for the final axe to slice through my neck and sever my life now from the one I knew yesterday. Eyes closed, so it's not really happening. And there I am standing in the line against the brick wall of our alley that runs along the back of the yards, the pigeon sheds and outside loos hiding us from upstairs' view. Apart from the window of Jenny McCauly's room, who we want to see us so she'll come on out to play and play down the line of us boys waiting to be men on her. And she will come once she's seen us do the boys first, as payment for being allowed to do her. And they do my bidding like this for years because we do Toby's bidding like we did for older brothers before him. And sometimes they still call into the alley when they want a bit and the pecking order changes and I love that and hate it in equal measure because I hate them and what they do to me and I love it when I can do the same to those boys further down the line and pretend I'm punishing them for being so naughty for wanting to do Jenny McCauly. By the time I get to her I'm not interested anymore and the fear rises that the boys will think I'm gay and I have to get a hard-on by watching Toby absolving the others of their sins. She tells me to hurry up as her Ma is calling dinner. Her Ma never calls dinner. Her Ma is where all the Da's go to do all their sinning. And years later me and Toby still drop into the alley to absolve any of the boys for the sinning they are about to do with all the Jenny McCaulys and their Ma's. I don't go back there now, not since our Ma died when I was twenty five. That would be wrong, it's not my alley anymore if she doesn't live there. People might think I'm weird or something, hanging around a stranger's back.

When Christine from HR walks in she sees my fear and I want to cry so she'll rub my face dry in her massive bosom and restore my masculinity as a favour for sacking me by letting me do her bent over the desk. Human Resources. Her mouth stays open and I know she wants me to punish her for bearing bad news by coming in her mouth. Her lips move and I know she's wet.

'There was an issue with security so IT had to take your computers. Well, not IT exactly, that's you, but you know, yesterday…I know it's untrue but this department's computers etcetera,' she says.

Not wet then as she trails off and no, I don't "know yesterday", or what yesterday has anything to do with my missing computer. And I know I'm meant to know so I pretend to go along with it,

'No worries, it's all backed up on the server and you'll have another one in here before the morning's started won't you?' I normalise.

'Umm yes well…' she ponders.

Umm isn't good.

'I came in to ask you for your laptop too. Routine of course.'

Laptop?

'Really? I don't have it.'

'What do you mean you don't have it? You always bring your laptop into work. It's a standing joke that you can't leave the job behind.'

It's in the car boot not getting the joke.

'It's at home. I don't bring it in every day.'

'Oh well, tomorrow then. You know it's just that, what with everything we, they, need it. ASAP they said.'

'They did?' they who? She's not very informative.

'They did. Oh and your mobile too please.'

Handing it to her then snatching it away to reset the factory settings, erase the memory and extract the SIM card. To buy time I say,

'I just have to text my wife, tell her I won't be able to contact her today.'

She's edgy now, trying not to say no, trying to say no.

'Yes, yes of course.'

Done. I hand it to her. She holds it away from her like it's a dead rat by its tail.

'We'd like you to stay,' she proffers by way of apology.

Phewwweeee. Relief of a thousand tons lifting. And then,

'You've been given notice, which is good. The extra money and time to look around for something. Or start your own business. With a pot of money like that you can start up on your own. Or just lie on a beach somewhere. Meanwhile we have to go through the nitty gritty so you understand the process and your entitlements...'

I miss half of the complications but I get the implication; accept the redundancy and go, or else. Or else what? It's hardly anybody's bloody business. Simply excuses for kicking me out the door before my pension kicks in. That's corporate take-overs for you, a scam. To find a lever to tip me out. They sent their scout looking for a reason, couldn't find one, so made something up. And the gossips have won with their curdled versions of things they say they might have seen. She drifts on, rambling about statutory this, breaks in service, training replacements who aren't and she slips into animated silence as all I can hear is the chant that we made up years ago in the alley, randomly appearing and repeating in my head, "All in. All in. McAulin. Mc all in. All in." And I laugh as I finally get it forty years later. She is startled and so am I by the inappropriateness of it, of both. She says that I'll need time to adjust. Bleeding right I will. And I say I don't understand if I've been sacked or made redundant or if I still have a job seeing as I still have to come to work. And she's gentle now, understanding, and soothing and soon she is silently mouthing words again as I imagine her naked backside heaving and bobbing as she tells me to push harder and harder. She snaps me out of it by sitting on the desk right next to me. With her stocking legs, crossed in that short skirt, just like two inches from my face. A sympathy shag please, my face says, and she starts patting me on the back like I'm a grateful dog. I want to slip my face onto her lap and start licking her, but she just tells me she sympathises and I'm brought back to confusing reality and the realisation that I still don't know what that reality is. I ask her again, about the job not the shag, and she talks about company reputation and I want to talk about hers and that Christmas party way back when we were still allowed to get hammered and have a good time. Before weddings and promotions and company regulations. We were just messing, had one too many I guess, queuing for the one loo because another lad had spewed his guts up and was sleeping it off in his mess in the gents. I was just bending down trying to move his leg that was wedged in the door when, as God is my witness, she leant down too and snogged me. The confused panic of stringing it out and stringing her out of sight and into the men's cubicle, over yer one passed-out. Then wanting the shag, but actually doing it? What if he woke up and saw, or I couldn't get it up? I had to think of Toby giving out penances and immediately I was there and I was hard and ready for her. It was awkward in reality, in that tight space. Getting tights and panties off, skirt up when she's sitting on the loo and she's lardy so just getting in between her thighs was hard enough and the bog was too low and in the end I asked her to turn over so I could get it in properly and I was worried all the time someone would walk in the jacks. She said she'd told everyone to stay out as it was covered in sick and that made me go really limp but I struggled on, pretending I wasn't and she feigned enjoyment badly and I just wished someone would appear and put an end to our miserable end but we continued on feebly until I had nothing to push into her and we pulled away awkwardly and I pretended not to watch as she pulled her massive knickers back on, God I'd forgotten them, and I made it worse by leaning in for a hug which she half returned half dodged. Only after did it make me wildly horny and now I'm ready to do her again, a proper hammering and a proper punishment for delivering the bad news. I touch her leg and she goes off in a huff. Bit late for that now. I think of doing her all morning.

I need to get out for lunch and still none of the team have asked what to do by popping their head in round the door and I realise I haven't told them what to do either and will the jobs get done and then do I care? Not my problem anymore. Or is it? I'm still confused about my role. I stand by my door listening for silence to make my escape and avoid the embarrassing looks. Everyone knows more than me. Probably know I couldn't get it up once too. Maybe not and this could be my chance to get some more from the sales girls? So I walk out strutting my ability to score and I am a stud magnet. They see me and drool down their tits, wetting their chairs. Mental note to sniff their seats. I leave behind me a throng of wanting women. I'm the man. Walking past the HR door I'm relieved to see it shut. And then crap, like magic, HR Christine opens it and tells the whole world I should tell my wife.

'About the job,' is she snarling, ordering me not to give us away? 'discuss it anyway. Explore the options for your future, together.'

The humiliation of that "go-back-home-to-your-old-woman" and there she is wearing tents for underwear.

'I'm sorry,' she says.

Is that consolation for the crappy sex, or the job, or the brush off?

I leave, deflated by her for a second time.

Cally

That's four times now someone has called the landline. If they wanted me that badly they'd have called the mobile. Everyone knows to do that. They can't know me so maybe I should go down and get it. But I'd have to run. Whether to get up, or not, how long to let it ring? Long enough for me to get there before it stops? It's been going for a while now, so if I'd got up straight away I'd be there in time to answer it. But now, well, I'd be too late so there's no point. But it's going on and on. Who does that? I'll do it at a run.

'Hello?' no one there. Dammit. Redial last number. Answer then you imbecile. OMG it's Louis' ex-girlfriend, Frankie. I can't speak to her. Phone down and why is she calling and how does she know our number? And now she'll see my number and know that I called her back and that's just weird for me to be calling her years later. Maybe that's who he sees every Friday night and not her next door. Or her as well. If there weren't all these kids about I could follow him after work and then he'd have to admit it instead of feigning complete denial and making me out to be a deluded green-eyed harpy. He would deny breathing if someone accused him of it. Sometimes he just forgets. Deliberately or not I don't know. But he does it so well that he honestly doesn't recall a thing. He doesn't seem to have much control over what it is he's forgetting though. Drink would do it. Like that time he found out the truth behind his adoption, after growing up as one of seven kids. In fact he was the only one growing up who didn't know he was adopted. He found out on his twenty first birthday when some smarmy git got drunk and got smart and thought coming-of-age should mean knowing-your-age,

'You don't know your real birthday do you?'

The drama in the detail.

Turns out his Aunt and Uncle Brown living across the street were his real mam and dad. Just give us a loan of your son, why don't ya? Mum Dad Aunt Uncle, depending on your information. They were bleedin' brother and sister making their bastards and handing them down the lane. They put his real mum, Aunt Brown, in Grangegorman asylum 'cause you'd have to be mad and bad to have done all that, he was such an ugly shite. He stayed at home on his own and minded her when she was allowed out in between her episodes. He was doing a bit more than that. Can you imagine, the twat? And they gave him a lovely send off when he popped his clogs down on the playing fields and all the children remembering him. Aye they remember him, of course they do, from the days when they ran so fast past the man, he'd be grabbing at you.

'You boy, come here, help me paint these white lines down the sides of your thighs as I slip in disguise it as a treat for your eyes lit up with surprise the very first time. It gets easy after that, you're in my trap of telling no one 'cause you're a dirty little boy now you've done it.'

'He was a grand auld fellow,' they said at the funeral.

So they all knew Louis' story, the stain of his birth, and they swept it away from him lest he was buried in their laughter. As they covered up their guilt over what happens. In front of you. They did nothing. The reality of his making was the making of him. He buried his shame until he forgot it again and we all know where that leads you. Nowhere. Thanks be to God.

Then drinking one night, Toby and him up for a fight and me in the usual place, in full-view hiding. The facts of his parents being incestuous agents rearing their ugly heads again. How did that come out? The eel through the spout of venom in a night full of baiting. Toby the fisherman, needing a hook to spear his brother onto. Jesus that was a good one. Having him pinned there, squirming in pain as he realises he's forgotten and remembers again. The story of his making. It left him so desolate, no wonder he'd filed it away, and here he is feeling it just like he did that first day. Should have kept it a secret to protect that little boy instead of giving him heavy weights to carry around for his life.

And now he has it planted on him to eat away at his brain forever, re-living the horror. For the next twenty four hours anyway. Until he hears it the next time. Again and again his eternal agony, but without redemption. Only infinity to go then. So when I ask him something, try to find out a truth, it's pointless because he doesn't know it himself. Handy that for him, or not, depending on the situation.

Like when Andi made a big scene last night about her Dad getting at her, some row over something or other. She was more than upset, so he must've been out of line and he completely denied everything and anything and I said he had to apologise to her because he must have done something to make her that upset but he just said, 'okay,' and then this morning before school I asked him to say sorry to her,

'For what?' he asked, eraser head.

'For whatever it was you did to Andi last night.'

'But I didn't do anything,' he denied at dawn, as the cock crowed, again.

'So you do remember something of last night?' I asked.

And he turned around to me, completely blank he was, and said he had nothing to apologise for. Then he spoke to her back saying,

'Sorry.'

Didn't even know what for, he was just being an obliging git.

'Sorted,' I said. And it was. I watched Cassie digging a hole in the grass outside, dirtying her uniform. Another one to worry about.

So when Louis walked through the door this afternoon, long before his work was over, I didn't know and I did know it had everything and nothing to do with what I just said about Andi, and his ex-girlfriend, and Toby's job. Two days of stressy stuff which were just the hors d'oeuvres to my incomprehension. It didn't get any clearer. He came in the house with his laptop in its case, as usual, and dumped it behind the sofa, as usual.

'Hi', he said, as he turned and rewound that sentence to put the case back in the boot of the car. Because he had a job down the country, by way of explanation for his early return. Which didn't explain it at all as that has never happened before, I shouted to my insides. Then he asked after what I was doing. Nothing obviously, but I always make sure to appear busy doing the cleaning the second anyone walks in. Duster hanging from the pocket, dirt ten inches thick, always something to be done, nothing ever getting done. He said he'd do the food shopping. Again, I was confused. Since when has he ever done that voluntarily? Threw me off-balance, it did, and into silence. He left to go shopping and when he was gone the phone rang again and the caller ID showed it was 'her' again. Burning to find out why and stopping myself, I stood there until it rang-out, going through the conversation scenarios that I was about to not have with her and maybe with him when he returned. I am still standing imagining all that, when he does return and another odd thing happens, in slow motion. It is just one small thing, but these things keep on happening and are piling up on top of each other in a precarious stack, giving off steam and getting ready to ignite or to topple over. I can smell the weirdness in the room. He pushes the table to one side of the kitchen and he fills the empty arena with a chair. Then he pulls out a second chair to face it and tells me to sit. The Inquisition. Before the interrogation can begin I answer myself 'nothing' and that's before I even finish asking myself what I've done, even though it takes ten years in my head. He twirls his chair to do that sitting on it backwards thing with his chin resting on his arms and I think how contradictory his body language is right now, compared to the momentous moment when I envisage he will tell me he's having an affair or was he made redundant like Toby was yesterday? But that's not what comes out of his mouth. It's a preamble, I surmise, and I let him ramble knowing how difficult this must be for him after a life-time of working in the same place and seeing retirement just around the corner and just out of reach as it's snatched away and he is cruelly dumped on the scrap heap of men in middle-age too old to start again. It isn't that. The mumble jumble is actually something he's needed to tell me for years, he says, and I haven't been listening and I don't know what he's on about and I have to stop and ask him to clarify as a way of seeming interested and concerned rather than ignorant and impatient. There is no defining moment with a neatly rehearsed delivery. It's a long drawn out mess of explanations with back-tracking and repetitions until I finally get it. And then I think, maybe even say,

'You aren't going to remember any of this tomorrow, are you, so what's the point? Maybe that is the point, Confession, Absolution, Move-on,' and I wish I could do the same too. To have no idea tomorrow of what he's just said. He's confused and I fear that this cycle is never-ending and that he's going to have to tell me all over again, for both our sake's. Luckily it's over and he is relieved, lighter for sharing his burden and me a thousand times heavier. Where do I put this new weight and how do I carry it around? It was his and now I can't give it back. I am overwhelmed and so I pretend nothing has happened because it is an emergency and because I have gone somewhere else to cope and I'm going to stay there a very long time indeed, in the back of my mind where no-one can reach me and defile me again with their news. If only it were just the one o'clock news and I could escape into the comforting sound of the weather report. Shipping off Malin Head, Fastnet clear. I have disappeared into my Bermuda Triangle, but there is no Met Eireann warning. He stands, pleased that it is all over and a little voice in my head says Frankie has being trying to phone him here and we both know that it isn't over and I get the next instalment slapped into my face. She's kind of like one of those Jenny McCaulys and I really don't see what she's got to do with it when it's not about any affair but about her telling him he has to tell me before anyone else does. But there is more that he has to tell me. It's connected to what he just told me, that because he did all that down the alleys, he did it to their daughter too. Their daughter? You mean her daughter. Oh God and then I finally get it, fifteen wedding anniversaries too late, and the Friday nights and the money given to her for holidays they're so poor it's charitable to give to those you know worse off than you and the hand-me-downs I know someone who can use them and why we never have any money. Now it's clear. And that isn't even what he's confessing to. No it's the bit he slips in under the door while I am raging about his secret daughter that I should really be raging about, that he did it to their daughter. When they ask we'll just say we fell out of love, because we can't say all this. We'll look dignified and do the same all over again. And I lock myself in and throw away the key. Blackie scratches around.

At least he's not been made redundant. And he's got himself a nice new phone. Solace of ordinary things.

Andi doesn't come home and somehow Cassie is here when I thought she was at school and needed collecting. Then I realise he had fetched Cassie that time he went out to the shops and came home empty-handed. I panic twice over that, the stress of having kids and now Andi is actually really missing and not answering the phone because she never does. Louis goes out to find her, catch her smoking under the bridge and I wonder am I completely losing it now that I don't a) remember b) notice c) lose two kids in one day, then realise it was only one. Worse still he has gone out for her and I can't change that now I'm stuck in here with Cassie. I try calling him only to hear his mobile ringing in the hall. I go to it, thrilled with the first opportunity in years to sneak a peek at what he's been up to on his phone. It's always glued to him. Because it's new there are only six texts and fourteen missed calls. All from that ex of his, Frankie. Or is she 'current' now? Checking the messages doesn't shed any light on the question. They all seem to be pleading for him to pick up the phone. Oh and here's one referring to me, she'll tell me everything if he doesn't. So that's it then. Well he did tell me everything, didn't he? I try to recall the afternoon's events but they are flattened in the back of my mind, in the black memory dump. I pick away blindly with a silver talon. Talos circling his islands three times a day. Finding little slivers. The splinters are a bastard to get out. I try to expand on them but can't retrieve them sensibly, because they weren't sensible in the first place. Trawling through them, fighting against the reluctance which so powerfully put them there in the first place and which keeps wanting to steal them away from me again, I am gradually stringing together sentences. His then mine, in the order in which they appeared. I replay until they are engrained at the front, this time, forcing myself in spite of or because of the lack of sense or any understanding around them. I am pulled-up again by remembering the fact that Louis and Andi are now both missing and head upstairs to read her diary for clues. Friends, boyfriends, anything, she never talks to me. Not knowing where it is hidden, or if she has one at all anymore, I plan to search through the detritus of her teen-floor. If only I'd picked a week when she was being obsessively tidy, although at least this phase makes her normal for once. I figure that if she's still stupid enough to write one at her age then she must be well aware that I would read it. Ergo she must want me to read it. I sit exhausted on the carpet of clothes. The mission is too enormous. I am overwhelmed by the task which is just masking the other thing which is already slipping away again and I have to check myself to etch it back into my brain in the right place and stop covering it up with band-aids each time it's rewritten into my synapses. I can't do this. And the yoyo can.

Andi

At the time I didn't know why I had agreed to meet my man earlier than agreed. It just sort of happened that way after school. We were messaging away and he said he was waiting down the road in the car for me, to walk on down to him. I wouldn't until he gave me a clue who he was in case it was a set-up like they did to Mary in third year, you can tell why by her name. He said he didn't remember that so then I guessed a bit more, that he wasn't in school and I suppose I kinda knew but wasn't sure so I asked if he had been walking his dog and he answered 'can I cum in your canal?' so then I knew for sure and headed down to the car which I already knew by now was his. I wasn't going to get into it but he said he'd just turn it around and swing down to the bridge so we could hang out there. It was all very normal so at least I didn't have time to panic about what we were going to do and at least under the bridge we weren't going to get up to too much in front of the smokers. Finding out who he was that day and who he wasn't meant there wasn't much point in avoiding him anymore. He stopped the car as promised. That's what I like about him, he doesn't mess like the lads in school. He offered me a fag as we parked up then put the packet into my bag on the floor,

'For later, please,' he offered kindly, as if it was me doing him a favour for taking them. He's not as good-looking as the lad in the photo he'd put up but, like he said, we'd never have got to be together if he'd used a real one would we? And, after all, everyone lies a little bit on-line, don't they, to make themselves seem a bit better? And I had lied too, or something to that effect, to my parents he said. We knew I'd be in trouble if anyone found out, for sending him those videos and watching his porn. Obviously it's not something I'm going to talk about to anyone and I said I want him to keep it quiet too. He said he'd be proud to show me off to his friends but he eventually agreed not to. What I really meant was the videos but it's embarrassing going there and I don't mean the wallpaper and I didn't want to bring it up again in case he wanted to start shifting. He read my mind and said not to worry he wouldn't let anyone see them, they are for our enjoyment only. Just for us and he's the jealous type and I felt all protected when he said that. He was so gentle and kind and didn't try to rush me at all. We didn't do any shifting that time, just being in his space felt like we were though. Dancing around each other while sitting still.

Being pulled into his gravity and breathing in his smell. I asked for his scarf so I could carry on at home. He picked up on it wrong but I didn't mind as he felt the same way as me. He asked me to film the carry-on with me using his scarf and that became our word for it from then on. We carried on for ages, just talking rubbish really, letting the magic wrap around us while rain battered the car.

'It's sending us mental with desire,' he said and he was right, the magic and being stuck close in the car because of the rain. It was so nice that neither of us could leave. It was dark and he broke my heart when he started the engine and said it was time to drop me back home. I was devastated and tried doing things to make him to stay, like putting my hand on the gear stick. He covered my hand with his and I nearly died. He smiled and said I was dying for him to kiss me. Instead he just carried on, driving with his hand over mine. Strong and a man. Or just a nice bloke with a cool car.

I crashed back into my crappy life when we pulled up outside my house and Dad jumped in front of us. Typical. Out of nowhere. Had he been standing there waiting? Whatever for? He tried my door, saw me, then jumped in the back. To get out of the rain or to give out, or what? So embarrassing.

'Thank God,' Dad said, relieved. Odd that.

'I was just getting a lift home,' I proffered, without proffering anything.

'She's worried sick inside. Where've you been? It's been

one helluva day.'

So it's about him then and not me at all. He asked why I wouldn't answer the phone and I reminded him it has to be on silent for after-school study or else I'll get caught and have it confiscated. Happy with the explanation he jumped out, asking us both to come in. My date and I just smiled and he declined and headed off home to wank about me, wanking about him, is what we had just said with our eyes. I ran inside and duly obliged with the scarf and pressed send. He showed me his end.

Cassie

Today I went to school. It was raining and we stayed in at playtime. Daddy got me from school. He was late and I had to go into Miss Healy's class. She said I could read a book with her but she read it all to me and asked me questions. It was easy. It had nice pictures of a mammy cooking dinner and the children doing home-work at the table in the kitchen with a nice yellow colour everywhere. I said I would like to live in the kitchen with a mammy like that. And the smoky bathroom and the bedtime story and pyjamas and a glass of milk. Miss Healy asked me if I wanted a glass of milk now and I said, 'yes please,' so she took me into the teachers' room to get me one. So we pretended it was like in the story and she read me another book when I drank my milk. I wanted to stay there but then Daddy came and I had to go. I said, 'bye,' and gave her a big hug and she said,

'Bye Blackie.'

Daddy got cross and pulled my arm hard in the same place. At home I went to bed and played happy families like in the story with all my bears. It was a really good game. I played it until after it got dark and we had a pretend dinner and did pretend homework at a pillow table and everything was a lovely yellow because I put a sheet over us with the lamp shining through. After that I turned the bath on. It got nice and smoky like in the picture. I told Mammy to come and see but she just cried in Andi's room. She didn't talk to me or play with me. Maybe she was busy playing inside her head.

The bedroom is getting smoky too but not in a nice bathroom way. I think Mammy should see it now because it is smelly but if I tell her she will just cry or not hear me again so I take care of it by opening the window to let all the smoke out, just like Andi does when she burns the chips. When I do that the alarm goes off and it makes me jump. I know that it's safe because Andi says it's meant to do that when she burns the chips. I run downstairs to tell Andi but she isn't home. No Daddy either. So I stand in front of Mammy. I don't know what to say or if there is any point talking to her. She stands up and turns the alarm off. Then she runs upstairs and is running around up there shouting stuff and stuff and I know it's time to hide at the end of the sofa. It's a bit smelly here too from the smoke. But there isn't smoke down here. Daddy and Andi come home and they shout about the smoke that was upstairs but I don't know why because it's gone now. Andi won't let me in her room to ask her why they are still shouting about the smoke so I go into their room to see if it's come back. It hasn't. They are by their bed and my lovely yellow kitchen is now a lumpy wet black bog with an orange bucket on the floor. I don't know why they did that to my game.

'The lamp,' she screams at me.

I think she wants me to switch it back on to make it all yellow again instead of that blackness. He pulls me away and throws me out the door which is a long way but I land like a cat and I think Blackie would be sad if I was a cat so I turn back into Blackie and I can't hear them tell me off because I am a dog. I go to bed.

Cally

We both look at the same charred, wet bed. It is what it is but we see two different things. Mine and his, a bed full of differences. Louis looks shocked, but he's stuck inside his head, probably looking at that too. I hope so. I don't know which is more shocking for him. I wait for The Reaction. He is thinking I made her do it on purpose. He'll accuse me of presenting him with this scene with the sole intention of winding him up, of exposing his inner turmoil, of pulling it out of him, entrails and all. Slap them on the coils and wind them around the bedposts. I won't let him. My preservation, his denial. It all goes the same way. He gets ready for the attack by getting rid of Cassie. She lands outside the room. He stares her away then stares at me. I pull a blank. On purpose, he bets. His eyes are burning from the smell and all the things inside his head and now that odour is inextricably linked to him and me. And to everything coloured black and everything that has ever happened. I hold his curses for him. Because I'm a witch. He looks relieved, sorted, brain-ache over. That was too easy. He says,

'It's so obvious I don't know why I couldn't see it before. Without you, my life would be bearable.'

He stops himself short in case I believe him. He is still staring right into my brain, after all. He walks out, leaving me to clean up the guilt. I battle to lift the mattress and to turn it over so it's only a little damp on this side and I fling a towel and a sleeping bag over it. I stuff the burnt remains of ruined bedding and teddies into the bucket, they are about to spill an Exxon Valdez mess again. The stress of kids is never-ending so I don't go there, into the slick. But I am so good at it that I hardly ever come here either and I'm beginning to wonder if I'll ever be able to come-to or if I'll end up getting stuck there forever, locked in or locked out.

Louis

It's a repeat of getting up in the morning and singing Angel of the Morning and another Perfect Day. Piano rolls in. Thank you, Lou Reed, for thinking I'm someone else. I'm good and maybe I am just what you see. Driving to work and I ride on through the day, a passenger on my life and I don't see out the side and I don't see out the side and none of it is mine...just on a dirty old road. I walk into work and get ready to get into gear and that's when I ask myself what's the point? I kind of don't have a job anymore but I still have to turn up every day and for how long? To teach some dipstick how to do my job so they can kick me out and pay them peanuts instead of me who's been here longer than all of them put together. How can I teach them what took me a lifetime to learn? They'll come unstuck, panicking over customers' problems and Mr Fixit here isn't there and they'll soon start losing business. I could set up on my own, take all the pissed off customers with me and be sorted. Mental note to copy all the client details before HR Christine Tenty Pants takes the laptop off me. Put it back in the car quick in case she asks for it again. Like she did the mobile. Now what can I do? What is the point of being here if I don't have any way of contacting any of my staff or any customers? And where is everyone? Walking through sales they all put their heads down to pretend they weren't looking up. Just do it and get over it will you. It's not infectious, being put out to pasture. Or is it? What's their plan? I'll steer into one of the directors and wheedle it out of him. Knock and walk in. Stopped in my tracks by a locked door. But I can hear people talking in there. Blimy all this secrecy all of a sudden. I try HR. No, it's the same story in there too, all furtive whispers and high security. So there's nothing for me to do. I'm really being paid to do nothing. And I'm pissed off about that because? I steer back through the sales room and Sandy stands up in my path. She's a big girl, like most of them here, she towers over me and extends round both sides of me. Built for comfort, not for speed. Tits down to her waist and up to her arm pits and really I'm just curious to see them, see how they work at that size when she starts rambling on about stuff and I decipher enough to get that she wants me to show her how to do my job. HR Christine Tenty Pants, stop calling her that in case I say it out loud, has given her a schedule of transfer skills to complete in order to facilitate a smooth hand-over. She's good on the old office speak. She turns to her desk and brings up my server on her computer. But she'll need my password for that. She has her own already. How is that even possible?

'Let's get down to it shall we?' Sandy commands rather than requests.

I'm still her boss you know. She goes on,

'I've been through it and can see some things flashing away here. Are they flagged as "urgent" by you or does that signify something?'

'Yes,' I reply. Obvious.

'Yes, as in urgent, or flagged by you, or something else?'

'All of them, depending on who it is and what they need and when the purchase order came in and their contract terms, and where the lads are in their schedules and what we have in stock. So you'll need to know all of those off by heart. There's about two thousand clients, some with multiple contracts, a warehouse full of stock and a team of staff. Not all can do all the jobs and they have their regions and rosters. But of course it took me thirty years so don't expect miracles in a matter of weeks. So what have you told them to work on today?'

'Me?' that terrifies her, 'that's not my job. I don't know what I'm doing until you've trained me in. You need to sort them out.'

'Can't be done,' I say, 'my desks been cleared out. Don't know what they're up to. Must be chaos by now. Not my problem. Or yours, yet,' and I enjoy the thought of how indispensable I am.

'So what do we do?' she pleads.

And I imagine six weeks of pure bliss, pressing into her enormous tits while showing her how to do my job, standing behind her and pressing my dick into her back and squeezing her forwards so they are squashed hard onto the keyboard and pulling her top down so that I can press her nipples onto each keypad, making QWERTY ever so lovely. She lets me continue daydreaming about her so I imagine gently pulling her hair to bring her face around and she opens her mouth and oh God she must see my hard-on now so I stop and concentrate on the concrete walls instead. I can thank Toby for that tip. He taught me how to hide the boner in case of an emergency. Like if some-one's ma came out down the alley. The Da's were sound about it, my Uncle Brown too. They just turned around and pretended not to see and never said a word about it. But once Mrs Riley saw all hell let loose and we weren't allowed any carry-on for a whole summer because she was out there every second of the day with her broom and scrawchy mouth. Toby set up look-outs after that. But that's what he said to do, look at the wall and it'll go down no problem. Been useful ever since. But I couldn't look at the red brick wall in the alley, it just made me see him being banged up against it from behind so I imagined a smooth, grey concrete wall instead. I could concentrate on smoothing down its surface to perfection. Works a treat. Brick walls have the opposite effect. I tried taking Viagra once. Waste of time that was. Cally asleep all night and there's me a stud with nowhere to put it. I got it in her a few times but she kept waking up and throwing me off. Not that I mind the excitement when she does that though. When she doesn't like it, it makes me want to do her even more. A bit more docile and I could've carried on. In the end I just had to keep wanking over her and in the morning she gave out yards about the damp and I complained she's a sweaty bitch and how could anyone fancy that. Dim.

I don't know where to start with this hand-over thing. It's impossible. It'll take me decades to teach this girl everything I know. I tell her I'm heading in to ask HR Christine how to do this and yes, I fancy her and this one, whatsaname Sandy and I've been thinking about Cally and Toby and I've plastered the Great Wall of China at this stage so I really do need a bit of sympathy, in her office. I try the door and it gives way this time and I'm so relieved I'm almost relieved on the spot when I see her squatting on the floor with a pile of files between her legs and I grin appreciatively at her welcoming spectacle. She shuts her legs nice and slow and turns away to hide her red face.

'We have to put everything behind us,' she says as I put it in her behind, in my mind.

'Yes, let's keep this professional, I lie, 'I just wondered if you could help me and Sandy. We don't know where to start, how to get her to know everything I know. She's only a sales girl after all.'

'She's very bright and has lots of potential. She wants more responsibility so now she has it. I gave her a run down on learning targets, so you just need to stick to your end of things.'

So no help at all here then, clatter tongue. What does she expect me to do, say I don't know how?

'So, this target spread-sheet thing you gave her, can I have a copy,' I ask her, 'so we're both singing off the same song sheet?' brilliant. Inspired move.

'I can't release personnel files. HR confidentiality and all that. You wouldn't want anyone reading yours either, would you?'

Two steps backwards. Ratatata.

'Tickle my back and I'll tickle yours. Again,' the implication works. Two steps forwards and she indicates that I sit down and she proceeds to talk me through what I need to do. It's way too much information at once to take in and it was her fault for making me so horny by exposing herself to me on purpose earlier so I'm not really listening and have to ask her to put it all into a document for me. She says she despairs and I offer to soothe her brow and at the time I really want to but she doesn't, telling me to just explain to Sandy the Operating System for today. For the week, I say, and she gives in so I win and I wank off in the loos thinking of her going up the ladder in the parts department for me so I can look up her skirt and see the same view as I got this morning.

After that it's plain sailing and me and Sandy get on fine going through the Operating System, once she's learnt what it's for and everything. After lunch we have to go through it all over again because she told HR Christine she couldn't understand any of it. Bright, hey? Meanwhile none of the lads have asked me what they are meant to be doing but I see from the Operating System that jobs are getting done and wonder who is coordinating all that, now that I'm not. It's strange, I haven't seen any of the lads at all. Usually I get to see them first and last thing and they'd be calling me all day. I miss that, and the banter. With Sandy it's just work and if she wasn't a bird it'd be boring. HR Christine asked for the laptop again, in front of Sandy, so I'm pretending I'd drop it in to her before leaving. Lucky she can't make a scene about it out here in the sales office. It's open plan. Everyone will hear and I'm getting that it's not something to be talked about. Like death, divorce and how much redundancy money you get. Talking of which, I still don't know what the amount will be and when I'm due to get it. Reason to schedule another meeting with HR Christine.

'Unusual name that, Sandy,' she looks at me confused, or condescending, 'I mean, it's not like you have sandy coloured hair or anything. You're blonde whereas my neighbour now, he's a proper gingernut, it would make sense if he was called Sandy. Blokes name isn't it?'

'It's for both. Mine's highlighted.'

They shouldn't tell you that. Myth destroyed and I have to put her at the end of my wank-bank list. It's like she's androgynous now, which kind of makes it easier to sit up close to her all day for the next few weeks. After that, what then? Don't think about it, it's too big to worry about, and the chit-chat continues while I fail to pass on my expertise and she fails to learn it but we carry on anyway because we're getting paid to do a job and who gives a shit if nobody knows what to do, it'll be somebody else's problem at the end of the day and not ours. Every now and again Sandy crosses the room because, she says, she has her own work to do too. Dandy job that if she can do a day's work in six ten-minute sessions. No wonder HR Christine gave her more to do. But all I see her doing is nattering to the other girls in sales who are looking over my way, giggling and jiggling and wishing I was doing them one by one. They turn the other way and are so embarrassed at themselves for fancying me that they have to ignore me when I walk past them on my way out for a fag. Another three are in a huddle outside smoking and run in sharp when I get to the outer door. I walk around the back of the building to see if any of the lads are around, haven't seen sight nor sound of them since I got let go. Jarek the Polish guy is just on his way out, tool-box in hand, headed for his van. He's awkward with me, embarrassed for me I guess at losing my job when he hasn't or maybe he's scared that he's next to go. I dunno but it's bloody difficult getting a word outta him. I'd be kicking him out of the door normally, but he can't wait to get away this time. I ask him how he knows what to do and he says, ignoring the implication, that he has always known what to do. I push him further, I need to know who is behind all this.

'Where are you off to now?' I ask and he says some old place and I ask how he decided to do that call before any of the others and he says what others, he's just going where he's told as always and he won't tell me who told him and he just jumps in the van and shuts the door on me. We were mates. I stare at the empty space he leaves and don't know how to fill it inside me.

On the way back inside I see HR Christine heading to our empty workstation, then zig-zagging over to Sandy. They both appear worried and spot me and stop being worried. Naturally they are relieved to see me. But I'm beginning to wonder if they were talking about me, if they are in on it together and are just pretending to be nice to me. That could be true because HR Christine turns on me then demanding the laptop and I say,

'This isn't the place,' because it isn't, not in front of everybody again. And everybody turns away their faces to pretend they can't hear her belittling me in full view of the open-plan office. And maybe they like it a little too, seeing me fall so they can feel a bit bigger themselves. Or maybe they know too. That maybe all their little huddles of nattering aren't gossip fests about fancying me and about giving me sympathy shags but that maybe they are tutting away about my dismissal. HR Christine has given them the low-down, her low-down, and they are dissecting it piece by piece and making up the rest until it is a full-blown story complete with headings and chapters and the full character assassination that they need to not feel bad about me leaving. I want to know what it is they are saying. I don't want to know what it is. I know.

Situation avoided, Sandy and I flump on, suspicious of each other now. If she wants my job then she's gonna have to drag it out of me, bit by bit. I wait for her to ask me questions rather than spoon-feeding her the information. I answer her alright, but just the bare minimum and she's too dim to know what to ask anyway. Like she says, she hasn't a clue about what I do and doesn't know what she doesn't know. She asks to see my job description.

'I don't have one. No such thing years ago, not even a contract.'

'But that's illegal, you should have one,' she says.

'I know, but last year HR Christine tried to make me sign a contract and it was full of new shite I didn't even agree with. Just wouldn't sign it.'

'And you can do that?'

'Don't have to sign anything.'

She was impressed and I told her you got to be tough in this job, don't take any rubbish from anyone. And don't give anyone a leg-up because they'll only bite and kick you back down when they get there. I was referring, of course, to my boss Murphy who has been remarkably absent through all of this and it was me who recommended him for promotion to director. He obviously feels too awkward to talk to me about it. Coward. Manatee man-flaps. Obviously not up to the job if he had to send HR Christine to do his dirty work. And Toby was right about her pretending to do a man's job, lifting her skirt to dish the dirt. So now it's me and Toby who have bitten the bullet. The others must be quaking in their beds at night, terrified of coming into work and being called into HR Christine and walking out a non-person. Sandy, right on cue for mind-reading, says HR Christine told her no-one else is being let go. So they picked on us. Not fair to hit the same family twice and she just smiles and says nothing and it's then that I know she knows and I damn well won't let anyone think that about me. I go out on a fag break to tell Toby the news, ask him what to do, but he doesn't answer the phone. Must be sleeping now that he's off, lazy bastard. I text him to come over tonight for a few beers. He will for a few free ones. He needs me. Needs me to cover for him and to look after him and it's me he runs to for money or a place to stay or for a night out or a night in and me who he treats like shit. Expecting me to keep our secret as if it's my fault, when it's really his. Always him who's done it to me. He never reciprocates. I just have to make do with remembering the others ramming him from behind as they push his face up against the wall. My hand protecting his cock as he holds it there and presses. I always know what to do for him, without saying anything. So I have to do it to Cally instead and I hate her for not being him, so I pretend that she is and I hate her for being him. He and I never discuss it, we don't have to. Now I want to. I want him to explain to me why he did all that, why he made me do all that and

I enjoyed it so it's his fault he got me started and he has to pay for that instead of denying it by not even talking about it like it doesn't even happen. Tonight.

Andi

After last night I can't wait to see him again. The sexting isn't enough, nothing compared to the feeling I get after being next to him. Needing to want him and in his absence he is all I can think about every second of the day in school, making it really nice to be here. I hide in the loos to text him some more and we arrange for him to pick me up at lunch time. But I'd rather do dreaming than have him leaning in on me. In real life. He has something for me, he says, but it's a surprise. By now all my mates know I'm meeting someone, can't wipe the smile off my face, it's that obvious. Grade A+. Next level. Check forum cheats for how to play. I have to say he's in the army, just back on leave, in case they want to see him and I don't want them to, not yet anyway. I walk out of school and he's waiting for me around the corner. He didn't need to hide like that. He could've collected me out front, I say. Maybe I do want them to see him.

'We've nothing to hide,' he agrees, 'we're not doing anything wrong.'

And we're not but God I really want to, I say, until he rubs my thigh and leaves his hand there. I love it but I'm embarrassed because I don't know if he expects me to do the same or what, so I don't. I just stare at it and wish I could get onto the next level without having to enter the game. He drives around, playing music and I laugh at his taste and he grins at me and loves me instead. The forty minutes is over and he asks if we can stop in the wooded lay-by to say good-bye and I think yes it'll only take a second but kissing isn't something he wants to stop, ever, he says. We stay and stay and keep trying to leave but it's impossible it's so nice, kissing in waves, he says. And I can't stop mid-round and lose all my dignity.

It is getting dusky under the trees so I check my phone to see the time and there is a text from Head Office. Mum, that is, saying school had texted her to say I hadn't signed-in for afternoon lessons.

'Crap. I have to go,' showing him the text, my get-out clause, 'and tell Mum that my card didn't swipe-in properly, that it always does that, doesn't she know, I'm always telling her. Never listens,' and I believe it myself. This time he leaves me at the garage, handing me a tenner.

'To get something,' for myself, he says.

It'll be credit for texting him. Glowing on the inside and guilt-coated, I walk back, remembering. What was my surprise, I text him, and he tells me to look in my bag. There's a packet, all wrapped up in the front pocket. In it is a beautiful silver heart necklace that opens into two halves, with a diamond in each to show our love for each other. I put it on under my uniform for it to burn a hole into me. I am impervious to everything else, walking home. It passes me by, because of that feeling I get from him. I don't know why but I love it and it's just so lovely I could cry. I remember his dark looks and strong arms, wanting to bury myself in him. Then stopping because I don't want to. And then I do anyway. Vacillating, it's called. Difficult words for difficulties. So I sit on my bedroom floor and do home-work. Not a strong distraction. I just think of him more. It's addictive. My first love. Not a fiction. Feeling fluid flutterbies floating through my belly. I write a poem to him called "Zephyrs Lightness of Tightness Of Feeling For You," but I only finish the title. The love-sickness has taken over my mind. I hide it in the wardrobe. And I hide it in the wardrobe.

Cassie

I move the family living at number twenteen further along the skirting board, to try out another house. One of the children caught lovesickness and they have to move again, in case it is contagious like measles. I use a pen to put red spots on the floor, marking the danger zone. I tell her if she isn't careful she might have to go back into the castle. She thinks she is sooo beautiful. Her mammy and daddy do too. They are royalty today, in their crowns, boasting about their princess. They get a bit carried away. Even the creatures living in the puddle beside the back door can hear them, and they get fed up and jealous. Andi comes in and complains about the wet. I tell her it is full of pretty mermaid creatures and I borrow her phone to film them. She says that I'm stupid and that mermaids are myths. But so is Andromeda. The fishy ladies are so annoyed at all the attention the princess is getting that they send their pet sea monster out to get her. He comes dripping out of the water, covered in spikey scales. He slides over the floor and starts eating everything. The mermaids can't control him anymore. He is working his way down my streets and gardens and trampolines, all of it is going into his mouth. He chases me around the kitchen three times. The beautiful princess has to be tied to a rock for him to eat and I run as fast as I can into the living room to escape.

Toby

I've been driving around for hours. Gotta call into Louis, he did ask, been avoiding it. Who'd want more of it? I pull up a few doors down and wait. I can see Louis' house and I can't see it because I see it every time and that's the problem, you stop seeing what's right in front of you. And I've a feeling I might start seeing again and nobody wants that. Or maybe he knows. Or maybe it's about me losing my job and he wants to patronise me about that. Or maybe there are a million loads of nothing to go on about but he will anyway because he's a whiny little emo. Something needs to be done, he is unstable. He could go off at any time and start blabbing, a radon leak. Cause and effect. My life is a constant guarding of our secrets. Protecting us, mostly him, from accidental exposure. Why put it into words when it's okay? But Jesus, he's going to spew it everywhere. I can sense his panic, the mad look about him, his stress

124

bouncing off the walls. Man, the idiot's going to snap and it won't do anyone any good, least of all himself. I don't have a plan for damage limitation. We need prevention, something water-tight, secure. I'm not exaggerating. Maybe he's just reacting because I'm the one out of work. The dick is worried about my stuff? No point treading where I don't need to. It's a relief when Andi runs down to greet me and I'm saved temporarily from Louis' impending whatever. She hugs me, a bit over familiar, considering, and I pull away from her and go indoors to my armchair. She stays in the living room and I wonder if she'll disappear into the sofa again tonight. She puts the football on. Weird that she's being so helpful and all, so I indicate with my head to scarper, which she does. I have this stuff to discuss with Louis and it's best to get it over and done with. He is extra nervous, or he's just having another crappy break-down. The last time he ended up in hospital, thinking he was having a heart attack when all it was, was a panic attack. I ask you. Needs to pull himself together. A pep talk. Brother to brother, when we're a bit more oiled and he's receptive, not so jumpy. The trouble is, he isn't getting any calmer or heading anywhere near to unconsciousness. If anything, he's getting more wired the more he drinks, which isn't helping. He's deliberately putting angry music on. He's getting cocky and confrontational, egging me on instead of behaving. Metallica, at his age? I can't put him in his place. Each time I try his hyperactivity just accelerates and I am reminded of his childhood and how we could've done with this ADHD label back then and given him Ritalin until he grew out of it and we could stop bashing him over the head for being such a jerk on speed. So they medicated Mother instead and Louis was just a twat who wouldn't behave. She only loved him more for it and made us protective of him. We made sure he never had to endure people's reactions. Though, God, we did want to react ourselves. Being closest in age he tagged along with me, so I was left to mind him, explain him, clatter the kids who wanted to taunt him. Over and over and over again. He didn't even notice. He'd just pace around like he is now, tottering on his jerky legs with the speed and memory of a gnat. Now add to that the anger emanating from him and it makes for an unpredictable show. It's not threatening though, I can still contain him physically like when he was a kid and hopefully he won't need that fist to the head. He briefly sits still on the arm of the sofa and by chance this is the exact moment when Cassie runs in and blindly takes a flying leap head-long onto the sofa intending, like she always does, to land prostrate on the cushions and watch TV. Instead she head-butts her Da right in the back and shoots him forwards, doubling him up and knocking the wind out of him from behind. The state of him. Both of their agonies are silent, he can't breathe and she's scared shitless. I lift her up and she smoushes in, hiding her face in me. Right glued-on, she is. He eventually gets up and roars, at my smile or at her, and she wraps her arms around my neck against him and we are ready to fight.

'I have to tell,' he says.

Ah, for fuck's sake, bleeding wimp. That's just him being a dick and thinking some good will come of being free from his responsibility, of holding onto what rightfully has to stay with him for the rest of his life. He must keep his lies to himself like the rest of us and carry on pretending. He just doesn't try hard enough. It's not fair that we put the effort into denying ourselves only to watch him destroy it all because he's too feeble to hold it all in. Integrity is all about being the same on the inside as you project on the outside. So you gotta change what's on the inside.

'I lost my job because of it.'

'No, that was me,' I tell him.

'And me,' he insists, 'because they know about us and me and them and her and these.'

'Shagging calm down a minute,' he's pulling miniature dash-cams out of his pocket and swinging his eyes around the place, like the lunatic he is. Wires and stalks. Luckily, for a cretin, he's always been a techie genius. We used to give him broken radios and stuff and he'd sit still for hours fixing them, his very own Ritalin. He's worse than I thought. He puts his face right up to mine, blocked only by Cassie covering my front, and all I can think of is how furry his eyeballs are, all yellow and red and I wonder how they can slide around their sockets without grating. The kid on me is his armour, not mine. Without her I'd have knocked him out seconds ago. I don't want her to turn and see him but I want her to leave us so I can thump him and

I need her to stay to stop me. I unpeel her and slide her down to the ground and away she goes. Freed and trapped into this, I follow through by putting my hands round his neck and push him away, fighting my urge, and hold him at arms' length. He pulls at me and says,

'It's both of us.'

It fucking isn't. He is the problem. I push him against the wall, lift him up a foot, dangle him by his neck. It's satisfying.

'You wouldn't dare. It's not just yours to tell, is it? Think of the consequences,' I can feel enough resistance in him to know he is trying to nod in disagreement, the shit, and see his fists clenched and his hate coming right at me. That's not something I feel towards him. I'm still minding him, even now, ensuring he does what's best for him. I drop him to the ground and he rubs his ears. Didn't like what he heard then? The Devil has been squeezed out of him and he's alright now. We sit down and carry on watching football, drinking, our discussion accomplished and understood. He strokes his bloodied palms, self-inflicted, self-pitying bastard stigmata.

Louis

I'm uneasy about last night. Not sure why, just a feeling and insufficient information to build on. Half a physics class. Past memories edited, partitioned off into another hard drive. Bits of data come into focus. Unforgettable. And others too vague and pixelated to recover. Compressed and hidden in blurred areas, fenced-off with grey crime tape. Both types are niggling because the one at the front is being hassled by the one behind, the one I can't see, so I don't know what it is. I just know it's a hassler and is trying to unzip and push its way out. And I feel bad and angry with Toby, Cally, Andi, Cassie. They are all creating and making me hate them for breathing in my space, for existing on the stairs when we pass in the morning, for eating the breakfast that I provide and for depending on me so totally, using me up for everything they want, never thinking to provide for themselves. Cally has done nothing for decades. Andi should be out working in that shop of hers and Cassie? What's the point? I didn't even want to have her anyway. Cally relentlessly miscarrying, trying to right-carry beyond the point that anyone cared whether she did or not. Like a punishment to the rest of us, so she could berate me with,

'At least you never had to go through all that.'

Yet I did, every time, until one worked and we got a premature runt that sucked the last of our feelings just keeping her and all her predecessors alive. Eight empty frames on the mantelpiece. I hate them all for what they've taken. My molars don't like it when I'm like this so I have to chew onto rubber to get rid of the feelings she put there. Andi catches me biting the spatula and sneers her teenage disdain at me. I pull the cutlery drawer back open a little, to annoy her back. It works, she can't not shut it. I repeat it. I will always beat her at this but if I stop she is not defeated so I am locked into it, which is just another way of her having a hold on me so I stop. Bleeding ridiculous, she is. She storms out and I've won. But it's too small a victory to let the anger out so I have to find something else besides kitchen utensils and her OCD. Cassie crawls in pretending to bark and it's only eight a.m. and, seriously, it's all I can do to stop myself from kicking her across the room to make her normal. She's not right in the head. I grab a bowl from the dirty sink and scoop up some old dishwater. Putting it down on the floor, I drag Cassie over to it by the scruff of her neck. If she will insist on being an animal I'll have to treat her like one until she stops and I shove her face into it, telling her to drink. Her spluttering annoys me. I'll stop when she learns not to struggle. Lesson learnt, I let go and she drops sideways onto the floor. Overkill. Overdone. But I'm too annoyed to check and too frightened that I drowned her. Just in case, I leave the room quickly so it looks accidental. I hear her shuffling. Relief and success are short-lived as she takes the bowl out back to bury it like a dog and bone.

I search for my lap-top for work and remember the habit is no longer required and that it's still in the boot deflecting the jokes and the gossip and needs sorting out before HR Christine does my head in over it. I still need to copy all the clients' details off the server before I'm blocked from accessing it. So I tell Cally I'm working from home this morning and set to it before Sandy gets into work and tries logging in and notices what I'm doing. Saving everything onto a USB stick, gathering leverage and insurance of future work, a life-time of contacts worth millions in this business. I log off the company server and hope Sandy hasn't been trying to access it, then wipe my lap top like I do with all the end-of-life computers before I send them off to my recycling scam. Tidy little earner. Now who will take over that job to make a bit on the side? Or fix the air conditioning when it breaks? Or understand the IT security system I put in place? Or answer the alarms at three in the morning? They don't know the half of what I do. I copy and paste until I have them all. Screwed. I commute into the office in no time at all. The stinking queues of school-run-mums are out of the way now the morning has started and it's a clear drive in. I walk straight into HR Christine's room without knocking and place the laptop on her desk,

'As requested,' and walk straight out before she can say anything. She should be embarrassed, taking that off me. I am. But she asks my back,

'Were you on the server earlier?'

'No,' I have to turn around now.

'Only we couldn't log on because someone was on using your password.'

'Oh? I only just got in.'

'Must have been Sandy so, getting used to it is she?'

'Err, yes, must be. I'll go see,' and I do, and that is how I get away with it and get my own back for being let go. HR Christine comes to see me when Sandy goes out for lunch. She has all the redundancy paper-work to go through. There is this catch, the bastards, throwing me an extra twenty grand but only if I sign a confidentiality agreement and a disclaimer promising myself away, to stay out of the business. What else am I supposed to work in, paper doilies? What a scam. Even HR Christine is sorry about it, she has no choice but to follow orders and to put it in. I refuse to sign. Twenty thousand for no work, effectively, forever? That's a shit deal. She gets in a flap about it but I'm not budging. She totters off to tell. I'm sitting on a gold mine of contacts and I know it. I can take them with me wherever I go. Oh shit. Wherever I go? I have to get onto that quick, before word spreads, that I'm jumping ship. I call an old acquaintance to call up some favours. We go way back and between him and a few others, he says, I'm sure to get a job. Especially waving my contacts lists, my dowry. He tells me I'm hot property in the industry. Aren't I just. The Heat Is On. We should meet for lunch, go through potential ideas. Go through my net worth. Word travels and an hour later the phone is jumping off the hook with the offers, it seems. Between him and the grapevine everyone in the business seems to know and is after me, flattering their way into my address book. That's a fingers up to this crowd. They must be shitting themselves now. They send HR Christine back to ask me into a director's meeting. I say I'm busy with Sandy. I can use this power and watch them sweat until they give me a decent package. No response from them, so I guess they are playing the waiting game and we are at an impasse. Their move. I can force a checkmate. I am your Bobby Fischer and Garry Kasparov. 'Dan yet navernoe,' was the headline. Yes, no, never, no. Then I can tell Cally The Good News that The Bad News will no longer be bad, but a brilliant stash of cash to flash around and don't even think about clearing any debts because I'll still be working and happy days, according to the Gospel of St Louis. And we all stand please to listen to the Word of the Lord and so it is and ever shall be, Amen. Kneeling in confession box and asking for forgiveness and listing my sins as stealing sweets and doesn't everyone do that rather than tell the truth and get murdered for the smell of cut grass? I haven't taken the sacrament for decades, still trying to think up some good sins for grownups. We are all praying down around the table, under the dim light, as I'm pushing a rosary through my fingers and going through enough decats to feel weak, Glory Be that it is. Sandy touches me gently on my arm and I get up off the floor and pretend I've found the glasses which were on my face the whole time and she kindly believes me and I want to cry. So instead I bounce around the office, greeting the girls so that they know for sure I am happy about all this, so happy I'm chirping and singing and it's a great relief to be leaving on a high. Don't feel sorry for me, I'm the luckiest man alive. Exhausted, I go to the coffee machine to recover. I don't know if they give me looks of envy, sympathy, ridicule, or revulsion. Women have too many expressions but they all look the same from here. How many times have I whiled away the time watching them from this coffee dock? Ten minutes each go, five or six times a day, five days a week, multiplied by fifty two weeks a year, minus three weeks holidays or two for ease of calculations, times by the years I've worked here. Divide by sixty to get it back into hours, and divide by twenty four to make it into days, and then divide by seven to get...shit that's forty-four weeks of standing here and I still haven't got a clue what their silent faces are saying. Clearly they don't either, if they can't make themselves understood in all that time. Jesus wept, forty-four weeks of wasted facial muscle, just making wrinkles.

'What are you looking at?'

'Nothing,' there to see, obviously.

I return to Sandy who is working away on the computer and I can just sit back a bit and wait. I suggest by-passing my security to watch some sport on it but she says she doesn't like it. She asks me how to do it anyway so she can book her holiday online and I teach her the process. Now I know that she is spending six nights in Portaventura with her boyfriend and son, end of May. I tell her it's an ashtray by the sea but she's been there before and liked it. I did too. Don't know why I said that. Got it from Cally. It was her idea to go there and then she slagged the place off before we even arrived. Ideas above herself. She thinks we should've been in Eastern Europe doing a bore-your-arse-off tour of the antiquities. Instead I got arrested on the beach, I tell her, for suspicious behaviour.

'What kind of behaviour?' Sandy asks.

'Dunno really. I was just drunk, trying to find my way back to the apartment when everyone else had buggered off. Scary, it was, those foreign police with guns and what have you. I thought I'd never get out of there, like those gap-year students getting framed for drug smuggling in Thailand and being locked up for sixty four years.'

'How did you get out?'

'Some ex-pat lawyer, always there for us lot, lent me an old suit instead of the Hawaiian shorts and told me to say "sorry" and pay a fine, bribe if you ask me, and he translated and all and I just stood there terrified I was being sent to some Gulag.'

'It's only Spain'

'Yeah well, bloody foreigners. And it turns out the guard could speak English all along because when I was leaving I said to the lawyer that I still didn't know what I'd done and the guard scans me up and down and said, 'for crimes against fashion.'

Sandy laughs at this and I feel she is conspiring with me a little, thankfully. She asks me to run through it with her again so she'll remember how to do it the next time and I ask her,

'Do what?'

'That thing, to by-pass IT's security, to go on the web.'

I have no idea what she is on about. She is making creases in her face. No wonder they need all that cream. I await clarification. So does she. Impasse number two.

'I can't tell you that, it's company policy,' I say.

'Policy, my arse. Let me try and remember it now.'

And she does, and she cracks it and I think she's a genius until she confesses I already told her once.

'I did?' I ask, kinda thinking that maybe I did, because she can't be that clever, 'oh yes, I did,' I lie and we are complicit in our defiance against power as we surf the net for shoes for her night out at the weekend and we find some nice ones for me too and she puts them in the basket because window shopping is great, she says, and for the first time I can see the point. How it passes the time a bit like gaming, but massively simplified for women. I suggest going into one of my games and she asks won't they know what we've been up to.

'Who's they?' I ask, 'they are me. I do the IT security. How're you gonna do that then, hey? Don't even know what a firewall is, do you, let alone how to bypass one?' I am smug, yes, and deserve to be.

'Is that how you did it? You know, hide it for so long?'

Again, I have no idea.

'Yes,' Master of the Universe, and I'm singing it and she joins in.

'But you didn't really, though, did you?'

'Nah. Just gossip and lies, gossip and lies. Did what? Hide what?'

'They say that you had loads of rude stuff on your computer, that it's been held in case there's a case one day.'

'The only rude stuff on my computer was emails swearing blue murder at morphing Murphy for his usual unholy messes.'

'You swore at him, a director?'

'To his face and all. Seriously, when he started-out here he hadn't a clue. I was literally wiping his arse for him.'

'They can't sack you for that.'

'No. They just call it redundancy. A streamlining of efficiencies. Recession proofing. Toby too, just to be fair,' blackmail does not discriminate.

'But how is that fair? Piling it all onto the one family? It's not on.'

Will they find anything on the missing office desktop? Nothing saved on it, I'm pretty logical that way. I try remembering but there is too much other stuff happening all at once, it's doing my head in.

'Where did they take my office computer again?' I ask.

'HR Christine had it put in the directors' meeting room. At least that's what everyone's saying, the reason why it's always locked now. Can't get in to find out if it's true or not. You should just say it's being repaired by someone else, not you, you weren't able or something.'

I head to the room and, yes, it is still locked. I've the master key on my bunch, how else am I supposed to fix everything when it breaks down? Louis the go-to-man, soon to be gone and then who can? I scan the room and there is no computer. I hope to God they have it safe, that they keep it. To themselves. I go get Sandy to prove my innocence and I say I put it in the skip myself along with the eleven other old computers the company were ditching. It's just a coincidence, I say, that I was given notice on that day. She is on-side and I am bricking it now because I don't know where the hell it's gone or who it was who made the decision to remove it in the first place. Not HR Christine, that's for sure. She knows a bit, but is just following directions, fighting herself for fancying me. Or was she sent to bewitch and beguile me. Smother me with her womanly ways. There are worse ways to die. So why? Is it coming from Murphy? After all the help I gave him, bailing him out, him weighing me down with his uselessness. He's threatened by me, wants me out.

'Are all your forebears green and blue?' he'd ask.

'From running?'

'And rotting.'

Out of his league. Slobbering there with his gall-stones and his gout. I should have slept with him when he was a green-bean, gorgeous and lean. No I shouldn't. Now he's a fat arse living in the past, borrowing from his out-dated reputation. No I shouldn't. But maybe that would have got my job back, the leverage of a blow-job and the secret way we pay. For it later. But do I really want it? I've got the chance to get outta here without any fuss. They're doing me a favour, it's not about anything else. I've just a few weeks of working in limbo then I'll be free, rich and hopefully not single, if Cally can hold it together. She took the other news pretty well. Knows what's good for her and well, she'll stick by me and spend all the benefits. That's if I tell her about the rest, about thousands of zeros flooding our bank account, about the redundancy money. It's me she will thank. Or I could re-write a future without her in it. Keep her just for week-ends, the dumb-ass. I'd hardly have to listen to her at all then, only go back when the laundry basket is full and she is desperate for me in bed and I can turn her down because I've a young one back at the flat who puts out for me the second I walk through the door, randy bitch or boy. Smack that pert behind.

Sandy pulls me back and into the open plan office where we resume the chore of understanding end-of-month billing, then constructing and monitoring of key performance indicators, until we are bored beyond belief and decide to check her holiday destination again for some light relief. She pulls up photos of people on the beach in their perfect bodies, not an overweight person in sight and we wonder how they managed to fill the resort with so many unreal people and where did all the normal ones go? Did they have security at the promenade checking their appearance and body-fat measurements? Are you fit and beautiful? Then please come onto the sand and bare your loveliness. Ugly git? Sod off. She goes into her email to show me some of her actual holiday photos from last year and before I consider snooze land she points out she had them professionally edited. They aren't unflattering, so I suppose it was worth doing if you want to kid yourself about your looks. I offer to do some for her and change one photo to make her slimmer. She is chuffed and wants more so we go through a couple of folders worth and I show her how to upload them onto a private shared server so she can see them later with her boyfriend. Me too, but she doesn't get that and they won't be traced to this computer. Not that it matters, she isn't naked or anything, just in a bikini. But I might take that off with some more editing later, share it around a bit. Services to humanity.

Cally

I return to the bedroom to think about the mattress and burnt stuff from the other night. It still smells in here so we are in need of new bedding. Coverlet for a cover up. I should weave one on my loom, using a golden shuttle, to make a counterpane for courting controversy. Lifting the mattress to inspect the wet side, I see it's gone mouldy black and as I drop it back into place I spot our old video camera under the bed. I retrieve it from the underworld and start playing through an old movie saved onto those mini reel-to-reels. It gets all chewed up and I pick another out of the bag to fill a morning watching memories. It jumps back and forth from one period of our lives to another, instead of progressing in an orderly fashion through time. Just like my perceptions. I watch Andi and her friend as happy nearly-tweenagers, joking with me as I'm filming and a barely two-year-old Cassie and there's the usual crying for dinner and family chaos. I replay it and see without even needing slow motion that it is full of sharp cruelties which are painful to watch. Cassie with that cutest little voice, all shrill and new, as she offers pretend food to Andi and the friend. They take it and pretend to eat this, in remembrance of me, then mock-vomit all over her. Cassie flees and they tease her, fingers up in riddance. I tell her from behind the camera that I'm filming her and she 'cheeses' the lens, smiles on static and framed, ready to be trained. I tell her I'm not taking photos, but moving videos of running around. Logic and literal and two she runs too, all around the kitchen. Stiff cheeses gripping her face. I cry as I watch the adolescents and their newly learnt sneers. Mocking her stupidity, as they perceive it. I thought they liked her. It hurts that they don't. She falls on the floor, declaring herself to be Spiderman. That was before the dog moved into her. She hears her Dad coming in the front door and she calls his name, excited. He enters and ignores her. Her face is crestfallen and my heart hurts. He has a big bag of sweets swaying in his hands. He waves them in front of her but says,

'I didn't buy them for you,' and hides them in the next room. She chases after him and what we can't see we hear and know. She runs back in holding a sore arm, crying from his cruelty and I cry for her even more now. And I cry that I did nothing then. The friend had disappeared as soon as Louis had come in. Always did that, I recall, and doesn't come over at all now. Because of him? The dynamics and the looks of disdain. The same looks Andi gives him every time his back is turned away. What was I missing there as her hate filled the space and he hated her back in return? I was missing there. Too busy fielding as he fired at me too. When he wasn't deliberately ignoring me or scoring me on a gradient of one to ten on the baby-belly still hanging off me,

'You're two years old,' he would say to it, my stomach, and 'you should be looking decent by now. Let me tell you a story,' like he's ever done that for his real kids, 'about this shit dinner I'm going to have to throw in the bin.'

I always noticed that.

Now I see the stories I didn't notice and even the ones written down. The essay Andi wrote in school crying out so loud she couldn't be heard. She nearly had a voice.

'Shocking,' her English tutor had said.

You wouldn't mind but she was nearly dead in it with the sex and the swearing and the needles in her head. How could that be written without an inside knowledge of a system of abuse in a family full of smack-heads who want children to release on? Instead of rearing them like normal people. Like us. She must have got it from somewhere. Trainspotting I do declare. A summer sat in front of it. Almost an excuse until he said,

'Not exactly age appropriate is it?' and what was he, the film censorship board? Not satisfied with that they got a doctor in to check her arms for signs of crack, of heroin, of shooting up, of rotting tracks. Instead he found the hardened scars of places where our family had bitten into her and left her nowhere else to go but on the inside, through the skin with a razor blade, to say hello to blood and goodbye to the pain that was sitting in there. But she didn't tell me that. He did.

'Counselling is what she needs.'

Bloody hell what counsellor does a child heed? Talking to an old man. She couldn't even explain it to herself so the attention seeking's stopped. Telling us when nobody was listening. Hearing it too late. Back on the film set Andi sweeps her sister up into her arms, free of scag, to comfort her, hug her. Holds her from Louis and the meanness that is steaming out of him and waiting for a break. To be saved. It doesn't come. And nor do I in the space of the film or in the spaces of our lives. I am not there. In his issuing of petty cruelties he's doing as he pleases. No protests and no consequences. It's easy when you're a monster. Cry. And I cry for us all back then and I cry for what it's like now. For doing nothing and for doing nothing again. So it's my fault is it that he's doing us in? What to do and remembering those two chairs on the middle of the kitchen floor and the mess he shared. The day my life changed. Except it didn't. Not on that day of days or any other day since. I do nothing. An empty game plan. On the African plains where the beasts are a roaming. And here we are, still sitting in the gloaming and needing something, anything, anything at all to get me out of here Lord do you hear me now? Isn't it time I found a fantastic possibility with an actual sense of realistically achieving it? Ask Louis, I would say, and lean on him. But I can't if he's the problem and I'm leaning so far in I'm about to fall over without my flying buttresses tying me into the gargoyles. But I can't leave she cries. The kids, the bank, the money, the lies, the ties that keep on pulling and saying I can't do it please. Leave. And there it is, he has to go. So no, I'm not. But he is. Let the Counter Reformation begin. All I have to do is say it and hope the explosion doesn't kill us. Well-practised at my timing after years of grovelling during those defining moments that we shared when he wanted me instead to be a robot on four legs and not a person. Now I am speaking.

I lay myself down in green pastures, so this is what I do. Psalm 23:2 with the power of Jesus because I have none, I call a neighbour, ask her to keep Cassie. Overnight. No don't think so, don't know you. Oh. So. Andi take her for a walk. What for? Sod that. Louis. Gets. Back. Kids. Haven't. Left. So. I. Say,

'We have to drive to the woods. To chat. You and me,' easy as that. The fear of the breaking. Anticipation of making, a scene. And I'm here in the actual event. So is he and it's no song and dance. I just say, when we get there,

'You have to move out. I can't let you stay in the house with the children here.'

'I know. I will,' he says, so I presume he knows why, but for the next hour he vacillates by, swinging this way and that and always getting back to the same place where he doesn't know that. Doesn't know what he did, is so sorry for what he did, he feels such a prat. Swaying between believing and leaving and denying and lying. Accepting and refusing. Entreating and losing. Please let him stay, he's done nothing wrong. Just work things out, you'll regret it when he's gone. Angry demands and tearful apologies for he's done nothing wrong. The nightmare you keep waking from and still it's a dream. You cannot get out of it because it's pulling you back in.

'You do know, don't you, why I'm kicking you out?' just to be clear, why we're here.

'Yes. Yes. Yes,' and he's not even near.

'Explain to me then, in your own words,' I ask, and he says it is everything good. Then he tells me of stories of things he once did, of boys in the alleys and girls in the hood. When he went with his sisters, his brothers and spawn, the ones he had earlier and the ones not yet born. His love of these babies is what keeps them apart, it's the one thing that drives him to show them his heart.

The two chairs. He is so sorry for it. So he does get it then?

'But I haven't done anything wrong.'

And we are back on the backtracks. Or maybe we're not. If he lost that gold compass while God passed him out. He has the excuse he needs. He reburies his guilt. It's there in his hands, covering the hilt of his gun as he shoots sideways and lies there. Remorseful and un-built.

'You are leaving,' I tell him, 'your bag is packed in the boot of the car.'

I'm driving him wherever he wants to stay tonight.

He can't go tonight, he says, no-one will take him he doesn't have enough money on him so go to the bank machine and we'll drive up to his sister Sandra's in town she's sure to take him in. Or Toby's?

'No, for God's sake. I don't want any of my family knowing.'

Even though they all do, because you were doing them too.

'Your ex then, Frankie? She's been in contact a lot recently hasn't she?'

'No. I just said I don't want any of them knowing about it.'

'But she's not family. And everyone knows about all this anyway.'

'She is, in a way, I told you that the other day.'

'Oh yeah. All the more reason to take you in then, surely?'

And then the coup de grace,

'I got made redundant.'

'You're just saying that to get out of it. You have to go somewhere while we,' he cuts me off,

'It's true. I couldn't tell you. I'm on notice. I have to train-in Sandy from sales so she can have my job and then that's it. Gone. Vamoosh.'

'Bullshit.'

'I swear on my mother's life, may God rest her soul, I was told days ago and I just can't handle it, can't believe it. You gotta help me. We're going to get a big redundancy payoff. Think of all the spending you can do with that.'

'Spending? You'll be out of work and no money coming in and…God what rubbish. I'm driving you into town tonight and that's it.'

I start the engine and he falls onto the dash, sobbing,

'Please? Just let me stay tonight. It will be easier for me to find a hotel in the morning. You can't just chuck me out onto the street after all these years. I need you to help me through this.'

'I'm not chucking you out. You did this to yourself, to all of them, us. And to me. Look what you've done.'

'Tomorrow, I promise, I'll be gone. Please, just one more night.'

And I relent to his begging like the sucker that I am and we drive home all red-eyed and as we walk in the door I am suddenly aware of what he is and there he is, in our home. Our children are here and how stupid am I to give in when he cries and how the hell am I going to get him out now? I hold the panic inside and turn into my silent action film. Steal into the kitchen and slide away his keys and hide them from him. Is he listening? No. So I circle round the house taking things that are his, quiet as a mouse. We are at this stage of the plan Sir, get him to lie-on in the morning full stop. Get girls to school. Drive him off. Now that isn't easy. Don't stop.

'In the meantime we will pretend everything is normal,' I say to him and he nods, his face relieved and I think this is what power feels like. Unlike before, shell-shocked and in retreat. I am all present and correct. In the moment and planning a future without him in it. Planning a way to get him out of it, a safety plan for my plan. Not to be rushed. A wall chart for its execution with health and safety at its centre. Don't turn on me. Or them.

I can't be in two places at once so I follow it, Louis, round the house. Trailing him. He doesn't clock at twenty one hundred hours what I am doing. Undercover. It's a sting. Make him like me liking him. It's easy when he's believing everything I say. I hold the truth. Hold back on the argument. The drama. Holding it all in. Then the rot sets in as the revolt comes in and the sick comes out. Up in the bathroom with my shadow stretched I cannot wretch and watch him at the same time. What a dilemma the trap and the cheese and how can I choose between either of these? When it's my children. Cry. And I pull it together. Straighten the seams. Yawling in my stomach and pumping in my ears, walking down the stairs controlling all the fears and telling him,

'It's a tummy bug,' heard that one before.

He wants something to eat, as you do when someone you love vomits. As you do when you control them and you want to make them ill. He's pushing it. Into that zone.

'Will a steak and chips do?'

He responds.

And the conversation flows between us and we know we will never have to mention it. Again. He thinks. He hopes.

Only until the morning, when I won't have to anymore. It's ripping me apart.

Yet how mundane, how normal, with the ketchup on the table. Life is Hunky Dorys and I'll take the cheese and onion. Stories. In the morning.

Chained to his side watching football on the wide screen and I rise for him to get what he needs. Whatever pleases himself, Sire.

'I can't hear it,' he says. He never can, 'get the remote,' it's in his hand to switch me on and off but the real one is buried in the garden.

'Cassie,' we both say and it's vile that we talk that way, together when I'm trying my hardest to split us down the middle and break the log in two. On his head. Then I worry if he ever had a go at her, like all the other kids when we were adults dating each other doing a line before that meant cocaine but it's screwed me up just the same as the crack would. It's not a party.

No it's bed-time, so what do you do? Do you sleep with a man who really disgusts you? Do you lie there and stare as he fixes his glare on the mirror, undressing you? Do I follow routine and copy the scene which we've practised for years, it's our marriage? We know it so well. As he combs through his hair, puts his teeth out and drops his trousers for the fairies to tidy. I lie in the bed, so rigid and scared. If it's not me he fancies, is it our babies? In the morning.

He jumps in happy. There's a word for you now I won't be using again. He is a condemned man. He is a disaster.

He will not stay here. There is no end to his laughter as he thinks of his luck at getting back in with his wife. He nearly lost her. In the morning.

Snore piggy snore through this endless dark night. I am left with their tails and my eyes staring brightly lest he ravish our daughters. Don't give me a fright. In the morning. I may not notice.

Too tired to end it when I should have. Too scared because I didn't. He starts kicking in the bed and words come scathing out of him, pulling at my face. He's jerking on purpose. Of course he's feigning sleep. The coward and the circus of him kicking me in, in the shins. Feet stabbing my skin. With his bony toenails. A marriage-map of sins, of bruises and scars. He uses me as his battering ram. He claims it's involuntary but he only does it when I'm naughty. I deserve it, he says, so I do. In the morning. I turn the light on as if that's any use but he yells at me sharply so I pretend it's a ruse to help with his sleeping and soon I have him soothed back to his cursing. Pretend not to punish me. When he finally stops I'm not sore anymore, just numb. Wish my head was like that. Stick it in a bucket of freezing cold water and feel the relief of feeling nothing. To be free of this, to be free of all of him. His voice inside of me asks me if I'm just using excuses to get rid of him? Shouldn't I be his wife throughout all of this and stand by his side and let him stay? Forget his filthy forays? Those marriage vows, for better or for worse, till death us do part, in the eyes of God. He will always be my husband. Always there, always around, always taking whatever he fancies. How can I supervise that for twenty four hours a day? Couldn't I be dutiful and married but just not live with him? To do that, to do anything, there is so much sorting of the things which make our life. I am kept busy going through them all through the night. I think of the times when I'll tell people the news and I'm struggling still with the way that it goes. His alarm goes off. I lean over and turn it off for him. I don't want him escaping to work early that's not in the plan. Get him out of the house he's a terrible man. Slept like a baby. Not the man I thought he was. The stranger in my bed. I vomit over the side. Pull myself together. Slip out and get Cassie ready for school with her sister. And gone. Return to the house I'm not sure what awaits me, how it will go, how I will make him go. He is up and dressed but not in work clothes. A sign that he's learning. A sign that he knows. That he's going. I'm too scared to say so I run up the stairs to get his big winter coat. Vomit, then hand the coat to him. Puts it on. Follows me now to the door, like a lamb to his slaughter. Like a whore. And we are out of the house in the morning.

'Let's go,' I say as we head off in the car to find his new life, although we have already gone and it's all too easy, it throws me being thrown a chance. Beginning to feel sorry for him, tears rolling down his face and check myself, remember what he is. Not too much, in case I throw up. We drive into town and I pull into a road where there's a yellow door for the homeless charity to enter in for the ones that get away. With it. Is it a hostel or just a private Georgian house with a weird front door? I Google it on my phone and I'm sure. It's the right place. To leave him.

'Get out then.'

'Wait. I'm scared. I've never done this before. I'm not some hobo.'

'I can drop you at your family's.'

'No,' again, 'wait for me.'

He gets out and knocks on the canary door and waits and waits and nobody comes. Pathetic. He turns and in a panic he'll be ruining my success I press the central locking. He bends down to the window and I open a slither of my safety. To him.

'I don't think this is the right place,' he says through the gap. I narrow it.

'It is. Just go down the street a bit and ask. People are bound to know where it is.'

'I can't do that. You do it.'

I sit. Stubborn. Ignoring him, for the first time in his life. He tries the door handle and sees I'm not budging. He is worried now. Part of me is breaking. For him. I mustn't let it.

'Down that way,' I point, 'I saw someone walk into the alley.'

He follows my finger and is gone and like a fool I still sit here and remember his bag in the boot. I rush to get it out before he returns. Leave it on the pavement my insides shout. He doesn't come back for it. Yet. Is he gone? I scan the mirrors for traffic wardens who would just love to ticket me on this of all days, the day my family ends. Louis texts me that he's in the right place. To wait and hold on. I do as he says, of course. He comes round the corner. Thinks the bag is his good fortune, to get back in the car, avoid the final cut of separation. He sees it sitting on the concrete. He's crestfallen and I really don't want to be doing this now and I do the worst thing in the world, I drive away and I don't look back.

With plenty of time to spare, I remember to collect Cassie from school, good mother that I am. So this is what it feels like. So why do I feel so bad? How did he go so easily? I explain his future absence to her by saying he is gone to help Toby fit a new kitchen and he will have a few sleep-overs there. Not a problem. She is glad to be home and I notice her skippyness, the joy of it and my joy at witnessing it. His loss. He texts to ask if we are still together and I don't know what to say, so I don't reply. We are, after all, married and I didn't ask for a divorce, just a get out. He is persistent, beseeching, then angry, then appealing and so he goes on until I turn it off. The landline rings and I answer, despite myself. It's not him, it's her. That so-called ex of his, Frankie, from his so-called past.

'We have to stick together, you and me,' she says.

Do we really? Why are you invading my life?

'Because we both did the same thing and let him carry on. No-one must know,' solicitous.

'Hang on a minute. You knew and you didn't tell me?

154

What did you know? I didn't know.'

She goes on about the past and I ask if that's why they split up and she says no, it was my fault.

'So how does that make us the same?' I ask.

'Because you are still with him, letting it go on. There's a word for that, complicit.'

'No. Unlike you I just asked him to leave. He's gone. So you are welcome to him.'

'Oh,' delighted she is, 'when did this happen?'

Digger. I put the phone down on her. She calls again. I ignore it. Next time it rings I pick up ready to bawl at her but it's his new mobile phone company selling a deal.

'I'd like to cancel the account please.'

'Am I speaking to the account holder?'

'No.'

'Oh.'

And I show that I'm rubbish at this. For forging phoney. How to get out of shit. Andi writes letters, I pretend I don't know, for skiving off school with our signatures written. Such skill at deceit. I need to get me some guile. I practise it a while, in my head. I think of going to the bank and siphoning off money, of destroying his credit card and getting the alimony. Devious am I now? A bit late in the day. When he works it all out he'll stamp and he'll shout but at least in my head there is a way to transfer his cash into my new account, using the passwords he sometimes waved at me. I am not as stupid as he says. But I am.

Curiosity killed the cat and makes me turn my mobile

back on. Full of texts and missed calls. I don't read them. A need to know he is sending them. Sick, that. I am full up and fed up with so much to do. So much parenting to be done and I'm here on my own and no one will help because I can't ask in case they want to know, in case they already know. Isolation. Turn in to the family left behind. Me and my girls. Are we devastated and sad or secretly glad? So secret I haven't felt that yet. But we are here and I remember the joy I felt when I first held my babies and imagined the futures we never got to live and I promise myself we will start again and do it better this time. Begin again, again. Just this hour to get through. How to occupy and try? And there it is, the simple act of doing is going to be my salvation. My sacrifice for others to avoid my eternal damnation. Make pancakes for tea. But it isn't Shrove Tuesday. What about it, Tittle Mouse and little Piggy Winkle? Go about my duties dear, they'll be ready in a tinkle. Why I don't make them all the time. Why I don't make them on Pancake Day. Well I'm making them now, and that's as good a place as any and all that. Love me for it, love me do. Grateful for having them, grateful for you. It would kill me to lose them. Children rolled in chocolate crêpes and losing the plot when I think of losing them too. So I don't.

I turn the heating on and settle in to tell Cassie a bedtime story, 'the Old Man of the Sea, Proteus, lived on an island and he knew a lot about everything. He knew so much about today and yesterday and tomorrow that everyone wanted to visit and ask questions.'

'Would he know about Andi?' she asks.

'You would have to ask him. But it would be very difficult because he got tired of everyone asking questions, of spending his life like some national library with no closing times. And he really didn't like telling people what he knew.'

'I like telling people what I know.'

'Stop interrupting.'

'Didn't the snakes lick my ears clean so I could hear everything in the future?'

'Do you want to hear this story or not?' finger to mouth, she silences herself, 'so he made it really hard for them to ask him. With his magic shape-shifting powers he could change himself into all sorts of things and was always sliding around experimenting, avoiding the visitors to his island. He said he would only talk to them if they could sneak up on him in his sleep and catch him and not let go as he turned into something else. And he could be any scary monster he liked, or any mountain or mudslide, so difficult to catch. And if they managed that he would give them an answer, and slip down into the sea. To recover, I expect, from all that. And he'd hide away, the god of elusive sea change,' and Cassie asks if they have money in the oceans.

And we stay in her bedroom talking, just rubbish about octopus banks under the water and how many cuddles you would get from an eight-armed mother and she says she likes it when I do that, when I hug her. Hungry for my litter. And there's my guilt, lumping along behind me. Go on, add to it. What else haven't I been doing? It's this wide. Tied to it. Tried it. Tired by it. Shattered by doing the right things.

Andi

Mum came into my room tonight and started off on one.

'We need to have a talk.'

Needs to go away.

'We did that already. I do know where babies come from.'

'No, I'm being serious, she said.

Awkward. Needs more practise.

'Me too. I don't need it again, thank you. Gross.'

'It's about your Dad…'

Not a heart-to-heart thank you. Not listening to you transplanting open heart surgery. What a shit load of stuff. She said Dad's been kicked out and I mustn't tell anyone why. Talk to her if I need to say anything. Yeah like that's gonna happen. Asking me to tell her stuff, as if I ever would. She's the last person. To do anything. She keeps on, explaining shit happens in families and boundaries and all. I've no idea where this is going or what she knows or why she can't just ask me out straight. And what I'd say. Nothing anyway, to her, anymore. None of her business. Lecture finished, she leaves pleased that she's done a good job. I wish. I text Toby and tell him some of what's gone down, the sanitised version without Mum's hysterics and I ask him if Dad has really lost his job. He phones Mum instead. Bastard. She's ranting around the kitchen half the night, mad at me for telling him and mad at him for knowing, when she's really just mad at Dad but he's not here to get an earful and she'd be too scared to give-out to him that much anyway, so she does it to me instead. Just like him then. I don't know why she's so worried, not like I want any of my friends to hear about this weird shit. I just needed to check a few things with Toby that's all. And he is family. Lucky Cassie not knowing what's going on. I wish I was a kid with no worries and no homework and just playing all day. I sneak out before Mum can carry on giving-out to me. There is no one to hang around with this late so I do a few laps of the park in the dark then sit on our usual bench under the lamp flicking a dead lighter. No life in it. It's really cold. Battle to stay. For every ten minutes that I sit here, I earn an extra ten minutes in bed tomorrow. I mark off each unit of ten in the dew of the wooden seat. I have got to four when I get a call from Toby saying Mum is worried about where I am. I'm okay I say, just avoiding her dragon-breath for telling him about Dad. He says he knew all that shit anyway and it's in the past and so what? I say

I'm freezing in the park so he says he'll let Mum know I'm fine and not to worry. Does she ever.

I mark a fifth stroke on the seat when I hear his voice calling me from the other side of the park. I say over here a few times until he can see me and says to come get in the car. He turns, assuming that I will follow. I want to. It's great when adults do the obvious, even though I could just as easily have walked home. I catch up and he stops to give me a big sympathy hug. He gives me another one in the car to warm me up, he says.

'Can't stay long,' he says, 'Cally is waiting for you.'

'That's a first,' I say.

'You mean more to me than you do to her. I'm here for you, you know that don't you? But it would kill her if anything happened to you. You have to be careful of her. Know what I mean?'

I do. I'm tired and hope I'm not turning into Mum who gets tired over the slightest thing. Like when she asked the neighbour to wall-paper the living room, to give her a few extra bob, she said, seeing as she's a single parent. Like Mum is now. You would think the house was being knocked down and rebuilt it was such a drama for her. She was so stressed she had to take double the sedatives and then try and stay awake through them for three whole days to watch the woman do the decorating.

'Why do you have to watch her?' I asked, 'is she going to nick everything?'

Of course not, Mum just couldn't be seen doing her

usual routine of sleeping all day. It was all go. She couldn't understand where the neighbour got her energy from.

'It's not normal,' Mum said, 'her running around like that all day, up and down ladders and working and ignoring your kids.'

Look at yourself there, I'd like to say. Cassie had asked the woman, when they were both standing still for five seconds, if it was really stressful putting up wallpaper and she said no, she found it quite relaxing. They were both confused. I liked the way she beautified our ugliness and I wonder why I didn't tell her. She wouldn't have done anything though. She couldn't hear me, not in the loud silence.

I ask Toby to take me home to bed.

'Did you drive out especially to collect me?'

He did, of course and I know he'd always be there for us. He must have told Mum to leave me be because she is asleep when I get in and it is forgotten about in the morning. It is touch and go, though, whether she will get at me or not. Firstly she was awake early, not a good sign and stressing about the lunches like they really matter. Which they do to me and Cassie, but never did to her. So I'm not complaining when she puts sandwiches in our bags and is ready to drive us to school and we are a) surprised and b) early and I remember I didn't get my fifty minutes reward in bed this morning. I think I prefer Mum being useless. She is a bit on top of me now that Dad isn't here. Ironic really, that she starts being a parent now that she doesn't have to.

Work texts and asks if I'll do a shift after school tonight. It's only after I agree that I wonder if Mum will collect me when I finish late, what with Dad not being here to do it and Cassie being in bed. I don't want to trouble her and then I get the brainwave to ask my boyfriend. I can't call him that because we haven't said it yet. He agrees. I knew he would. Says he'll take me in also, collecting me early from school so we can have some time together. Depend on him. Plus there's no third degrees, just accepts me for who I am. Grateful to be with me too, he tells me. Flattery. And easy to be with and he can put stuff into words like I never can. We drive up to the plains so no-one will see us and pull into the lay-by where everyone else who doesn't want to be seen goes to hide and we can all see each other. He says he doesn't want to rush me so I'm honest and tell him I want to get it over and done with, not saying the bit that I want to get out and go back in time two hours or three hundred years. And how did we get to here anyway? When he tries and I don't, he says I'm a tease like it's an insult and I can't get out of it now. Virgin loser. Wondering if he knows. If he can tell. He doesn't say that it's obvious. Getting away with it and too far in to get out of it again. And I can't put stuff into words. I said that already. See? So I have to. We do it in the back of the car with me sitting on top of him so I can control it, he says. I do and it's okay when it's done. And I feel let down. By me or him. And I've achieved something. Mission accomplished. It was awkward and now I have to go into work and clean myself up. He offers to drive me back to his mate's where he's staying to use the bathroom there and I ask why the hell didn't we go there in the first place?

'I thought it would be intimidating for you,' he explains, without explaining anything at all. But it is when we go in. The weird shit atmosphere bending the walls when I see his friend's bare back through a door. He's shagging on a bed with one leg on the floor. No one speaks. The sound of bodies squelching and a mattress bouncing. I concentrate on the bed instead. It must be ten foot four, it's massive. And, as in Mass, the two of us stand there and wait. I'm supposed to look at them, like he is? I'm supposed to know which is more awkward, me being here or me knowing the girl that is getting a doing? This is what grown-ups do. She was at my school until her mum died, then she disappeared into that awkwardness of grief but here she is now. Howya doin? or I was sorry to hear, neither is appropriate now I'm looking up her backside. She's holding onto the bed-rails like they're saving her life and she mustn't let go. Then I see that she can't, she is handcuffed to the things. Guilty intrigue for observing her sins.

'Water bed,' my fella says.

'What a bed.'

'Will we join them?'

'No,' to be brave. Unsure. They don't even turn and say hello. How to navigate this? I don't know. This is what grown-ups do. My boyfriend is breathing really hard and I feel he wants me but I'm out the back-yard burying bad boring sentiments before looking the part. I can do this, but I can't. He guides me down the dim, wide, wood-panelled corridor to safety, for privacy or something or other. His room is so huge. Why do they have an apartment like this? It's ancient, un-lived in, expansive, it's shit. I don't like this, I want to say but I don't want to look like a twit who's out of her depth and just needs to learn how to do it. I stand there looking at another enormous bed. I'm out of my depth. With the furniture. He goes to the bathroom, my reason for coming here. I wait my turn. For what? In the massive low-lighted quietness. The weight of experience waiting to happen. He lifts me the way I pick up little sleeping Cassie and he places me down, stroking my hair and holding my face. Gorgeous and softly, he goes at my pace this time. Making him lovely, he makes my heart race. We have proper sex, with him on top of me and all, and it's nearly normal and it's that which I keep remembering afterwards, but wrapped in that weirdness of the flat.

All through my shift, when I'm working, I'm thinking of shifting with him and I really want that nice bit again, knowing I'm changed. I'm grown up. Weird, but the same. Guilty missionaries' missions. My shop supervisor sends me to work in the stock-room out back, my face is too red customers will think it's a rash. I'm off-putting? She puts me on unpacking duty. It all comes out. Until the sales lad comes in with his excuses for being there and his acne and he fancies me, doesn't he always, and I stand on the packing boxes and look down on him, from the height of my new knowledge. He tries it on again but I'm a woman now and I tell him my boyfriend will kill him and he leaves me alone to my adulthood. Sorted. At closing time I prove my superiority with said boyfriend who comes to collect me. He has a car. He says he wants to cum again.

'Not yet though, that would be strange,' I say, deferring more sex or that flat or what it contains. That odd place staining my head with images of being strapped to the bed.

'I'm not up for it again either. Gotta rest the old man,' he says.

I'm not sure if he means his dick or himself, but I'm relieved anyway. See it as a kindness for not pushing me, I think I said. I look at him differently after the night we've just had, for treating me gently. I went along. I'm not sad. Just empty. And bad.

Cassie

I look for Daddy, when I remember to. I have to say sorry because I nearly killed him with my head and now he can't come back. I tell my teacher he broke his back and all of our class prays for it. I don't tell her it was my fault, that I was running too fast or that Uncle Toby caught me and that they both wanted me and didn't want me and shouted at each other. I don't know if that is a good or bad thing to tell at morning circle time. Emily is sitting next to me and she passes me Travelling Ted after telling us all about how she went to swimming lessons with him last night. I say teddies can't swim and we have an argument about that and I have to turn around and say, 'sorry,' I'm not. They can't swim. She had drawn a rubbish picture of him in the water. It looks like a messy blue rat. I am sick of saying sorry. I get made to say it again after lunch because Aidan from junior infants wets the floor during PE and blames me for it and my skirt is all wet with his pee after I sit in it, so everyone believes him. It's not fair. He even tried to take Travelling Ted off me, even though it's my turn to have him for the night.

On our way home from school Mammy brings us through the park so I have a story to tell tomorrow about Travelling Ted. I drop him down the slide and hold him on the zip-line and the swings and wish she would do that for me too. She won't even go on the roundabout, she has her phone she has to look at. I build a den in the tunnel for me and Travelling Ted to hide in, looking out of the end towards the playing fields on the other side of the fence. There are two people walking across the pitches in straight lines, pushing a box on wheels. It flaps along, leaving white behind it. They puff and laugh and smoke comes out of their mouths because it is so cold. Me and Travelling Ted watch another man picking up litter around the edges. He has a bright yellow vest on and he has a stick that does all the picking-up for him. We crawl out and go through the broken gap to his side. We ask him if we can help. I just want to try the stick thingy really. He puts his hands around mine and Travelling Ted's to show us how it works. He tells us we can collect all the bits around the bench while he has a sit down. Travelling Ted picks up loads of litter for him and puts it in the bin liner, which he holds open.

'Miss will be proud of you at school Travelling Ted,' I have to praise him.

The man says that's a good name and asks me what

mine is. I tell him it's short for Cassandra who is a famous Greek myth.

'Are you for real?' he asks.

'I am, but no one can see me and I have to tell the truth.'

'Always,' he says, 'come sit up here beside me.'

The flapping box stops. It has come to a mound, just like one of my cairns. I ask the man sitting next to me what is buried under it. He says, 'moles,' and explains that they are little black furry animals who live in the dark, underground.

'You're mean!' I tell him and we run back through the fence to our tunnel and spy on him until he has gone. Blackie growls after him. We would never bury anything alive. Mammy shouts across the playground to stop barking. At home I draw the picture about Travelling Ted's day. I want to show the poor moles under the mud but it just looks like a brown and black shiny scribble, worse than Emily's. I press harder to make it look darker down there and I rip out holes to make their eyes. Mammy says it really does look like The Underworld and she tells me all about a monster who lives there and you need bits of string to get out. She doesn't have any. She pretends she isn't crying.

Cally

Exhaustion is in here instead of Louis. His way of controlling me in his absence or maybe it's a divine punishment for telling him to leave? It's relentless, being made to do all this on my own. I'd almost take him back, without the bad bits of course. An overwhelming point. I need help. I text everyone in my contacts.

Me: just asking all my good friends out there
           if any of you can help me out with child
           care at this... difficult time.

Genius. I wait. Nothing comes in. I get one telling me about a great childminder she knows for a fiver an hour. That's not what I meant. She should know I need it for free. I show it to Andi and she asks, apart from sounding like someone died, why am I broadcasting it to everyone I know if it's supposed to be such a big secret? I hadn't thought of that and why hasn't anyone asked what's up?

'How many of those are actual friends Mum? You've never had any friends.'

'I have. I did. Once. I have their numbers,' she's right. That's all I have left.

A second text ignores my SOS but is a lifeline of sorts. It's from an old friend who stopped being an actual friend years ago except we still think we are by sending cards at Christmas and saying how time flies and that we must catch up. But I'd be too embarrassed to do that now and what have I got to show for a lifetime of being so busy? It was an invite to turn up with all our old crowd of girls at her fortieth birthday party tonight and obviously I won't go because I'd either cry or throw up. Andi reads it and tells me I should go, when did I last have a night out on my own? And I can't tell her when that was because it was so long ago that I doubt that I ever did. She's on my case to attend and the thought of it is terrifying, all those pals from the past who married well or went to college or got careers and nice houses and a husband they got to keep because they did everything right and I didn't. Not anymore.

'But they don't know that,' points out Andi, 'unless you tell them.'

And I think about the story of my life as I would like it to have been told and that is the story I would like them to hear. How will they know any different? So Andi persuades me and is already throwing outfits at me when I spot the ulterior motive,

'My boyfriend,' she starts, knowing I am starving for her confidences, 'he's lovely, really kind. Mind if he calls over tonight, to keep me company in case Dad tries turning up and does something stupid?'

I want to dig for more information and have to hold back in case she withdraws. Yet I want to yell at her for her brazen manipulation.

'Yes sure. I didn't want to go out anyway.'

'Mum!'

And I have lost the mother daughter thing we almost had going there unless I cave into her and then it's just the daughter thing.

'Alright. I'll go,' and I am amazing and useless at the same time. This is new to me, so be kind.

I get a taxi into town and meet up for the reunion of all of our pasts and each time one of them talks about their present I remember what Andi said about them making up their own stories anyway and I add my bit of fiction to the literary event of middle-aged women being what they think each other is, but probably isn't. We're all secretly living fucked-up lives, I hope. We must do this again, knowing we never will. Going home three of us realise we are heading back the same way and decide to retrace our steps by taking the bus just like we did on Saturday nights in our twenties when getting pissed was a laugh. Emboldened by each other, no it was the Vodkas stupid, we giggle through the queues asking which bus goes where until we find the right one and we pile onto the back seat, hysterical that we are still hysterical. There were no 'auld ones on the back seat back in our day. They were tucked up in their curlers in bed, being of service. They jump off their husbands as they jump off the bus, landing on nice streets and I wonder if they did that just to show off and then have to walk the two miles to their Bovis home estates, or if they really are that loaded? I'm travelling out of their swanky post-codes now and it shows. Gaudy take-aways, rowdy revellers puking into bins and tarts picking fights with each other. It's feral and wonderful. The bus stops at traffic lights and I watch three men huddled around a table in a late-night cafe, large with their layers of padding ready for a life on the streets while growing smaller on the inside. Then I realise that one of them is Louis, just as the other two get up to leave. I feel sad at how lonely he is in there, drinking tea from a paper cup, his entire life inside it. Suddenly his two friends are getting on the bus and staring at me down the aisle. He has told them of my betrayal and they project his hatred at me, blaming me for making him homeless, forcing him to sit in rotten cafes at one in the morning to buy some time indoors before sleeping in the gutter under cold cardboard. They despise me for being their wives. Louis turns towards the bus just as the lights change and we pull away and it isn't him.

In strange places faces look like the people you know, except I'm not in a strange place and I keep seeing Louis everywhere. And he is nowhere. My guilt and his guilt make me feel sick again. It's that horrible feeling that sits there because it's nowhere else to go and I don't know what to do with it and I've been hiding it all night so God give me a break and just take my life away will you? Sick spews out. Now everyone will leave me alone. I feel like I'm sitting in that cafe on my own.

I get off at the next stop and a while later I phone Toby,

'Can you come and pick me up? I'm at the garage. Long story,' he agrees, obviously, and when he turns up I make the mistake of telling him I got off at the wrong bus stop.

'How so?' he asks.

'I was the last of our gang left on the bus and it was dark. And I'd just thrown up all over the seat next to me and had to move down, so I didn't see our stop coming and next thing we were somewhere I didn't know and had to get off and walk back until I recognised somewhere but I just didn't. I was walking all over the place. Walking normally, not swaying or anything like that and a car full of people stopped to ask if I was alright and they showed me the way.'

'Whoa slow down. You didn't get in with strangers?'

'Of course not. They were very nice. Must've been on their way back from a party, just doing a good deed,' I think about it and, 'they could have been off-duty police,' I say.

'Either way, you were nearly abducted or nearly arrested. You gotta be more careful. It's risky, could've got nasty wandering around late at night pissed out of your mind, anything could've happened.'

'Ah come off it. It was only a fortieth. I'm fine, I just got lost, that's all.'

'Yeah but it makes things difficult, and I don't mean right now. It scares your kids when you drink or else you go to bed and neglect them.'

'My kids are great thank you very much, you should apologise for that.'

'And yet,' Toby says, 'isn't it strange how you selectively heard what I just said. That you only hung onto feeling hurt over your kids, while totally fucking failing to see my point.'

'Which is?'

'That you need to stop drinking and take care of them. And yourself. Is it the way I talk, or do you just choose which bits to understand?'

The latter, he thinks, when I turn it back on him by recounting the number of cans he's had this week.

'So you've got a tally board and if I'm worse than you then you can't have a problem too?' he asks.

'I do have a problem. It's you.'

'My point exactly. And it goes right over your head.'

He drops me off at my house and drives away.

Andi

Dad's been texting me, mostly to say he loves me and to kiss Cassie and stuff. Stuff he never does in real life, unless he's pissed and then he goes right over the top. Thinks it's funny. It isn't. Because I'm cranky on hormones, he says. Because he loves me. Because he loves himself. Says he's stayed at Frankie's house which is weird because she's his ex-girlfriend and didn't he have a kid with her years ago? Another daughter gets him instead of me but then I'm glad she gets him instead of me and then I'm not and it goes around in circles and I just wish they'd sort their shit out and not involve me. He asks if we'll meet up in town so he can see me and I say yes because I want to and I don't want to and I know Mum will go mad and I'm going mad going between the two of them. If they were just in one place and normal again. I have to get the bus with Cassie when Mum goes off for her night out. And I miss the chance of having my boyfriend round, she even said yes, but I had to choose the lesser of two truths. And I can only chicken out of one. I bring a bag of things Dad asked for and convince Cassie that we're going on a secret night-time adventure.

'In my pyjamas?' she asks.

See what they've driven me to. And then she's a pain to drag along, she's so tired and over-excited. We get wet in the freezing rain waiting for the bus, waiting for him, wanting a Dad, hoping it's him, just not him. Then we get tutted at by some old hag for being out late or she thinks I'm a teenage mum and should've known better than to get pregnant and get on a bus displaying my wanton sins. I get that a lot when I'm out with Cassie. God help the real wanton sinners. Dad said he'd meet us at the bus station and I begin to panic that Mum might see us in town so we wait ages before getting off and the driver actually tells us to get off, then looks worried and I worry he's going to report us. For what, for crappy families? Dad is there at the back of the station and waves to us so the driver is happy he can ignore what he didn't just see and it carries on. You'd think I was carrying a sack of gold the way Dad reacts to the hold-all. Holds more than us. Cassie wishes she was the bag because he ignores her and I think what a bloody waste of time it was us sneaking out here to see him. Parcelforce would've done the job. She squats on the floor panting. No reaction. Left wanting. I persuade him to get us a McDonalds and while Cassie squirms around on the plastic seats he starts asking me stuff about Mum and

Cassie wants to know why he wanted to leave and is his back better?

'I didn't want to leave. Your Mum chucked me out.'

'Why?' Cassie asks.

'Because of Andi there,' nodding in my direction, 'she says I did things I shouldn't.'

'I didn't,' I defend myself from splitting up our family and making us fatherless and all that he implies, 'just that night, that's all,' and the rest.

'Yes and I didn't do anything, did I?'

'Eeeww Dad, Cassie's here.'

'Well then. And all this has happened because of that one night when nothing happened.'

But it did. It always does. Going mad. Never enough. To blame him. Only me. He doesn't see.

'Mum said a whole load of other stuff too about you being down alleys with some girl you got pregnant years ago and that the baby is even older than me now and you're still seeing her mum Frankie and you kept going to the alleys until you married and you were like ancient then.'

'Bullshit. I knew she'd be turning you against me now she's kicked me out so she can get my house off me and take everything I've ever worked for. Look I'm sitting here with nothing except this bag. Nothing. She's taken it all, even you two and filled you up with all these lies.'

I hope Cassie doesn't understand it all. The man

leaning against the dividing banquette does. Like everyone, he doesn't know who to believe and prefers Dad's version, because women are evil bitches and men are never wrong, so that makes me full of make-believe. And that makes me mad, that he can turn it on me by saying it's all my fault. He doesn't get how pissed I am at him for that. And I can't tell him because for him it was no big deal and I'm just not allowed to explain it. Even if I was able to, I would be squashed.

Dad says he'll come back with us on the bus. I am of no consequence then? I am annoyed at myself for coming, for wanting a Dad. Instead I say,

'Well what was the point in that then, I could've stayed at home the whole time?'

'I needed the keys and the money youbrought me.'

'You could've come to the house for them.'

'I didn't know then that Mum'd be out.'

'What difference does it make, if you are coming back anyway?'

'None,' he says, like there isn't, like I don't matter.

'Will Mum mind that you go back or will she go mental?'

'She will mind. She will go mental. Then she'll be glad. You know what she's like. She's just waiting for me to make the first move and we'll be back together again in no time. It will all be fine.'

For him. I want him to come home but I don't and now I feel like I've done something wrong by doing him some good and anyhow he's my Dad and we've just been on a family outing and I want that bit of him, just not all the other bits. Sieve my life.

'I wish I was five.'

Louis

'So if you're fourteen now...'

'I am fourteen now.'

'And if your mum is three times older than you...when you're fifty, she'll be in her eighties. That's only a third older than you then. How can the difference shrink?'

'Because we all turn into our mothers. Small insignificant others, invisible women. We're all the same to you.'

'Yeah. That first bit.'

'And the rest.'

'You're getting more like her alright. Get yourselves upstairs to bed,' and I squeeze her friendly behind, friendly like, but she minds instead of letting me take my time and, 'I was only pushing you up,' I shout after her and I find myself annoyed again. I pace around the home I almost lost, noticing things of mine have been removed, replaced by Cally's frostiness. Turning the furniture against me in her scheme to rearrange our life. The witch thinks she can screw me over, well she can't. This is mine and I'll beat her this time. In more ways than one. She either stays and does as she's told and I can't finish that sentence before I am swamped with the vision of her naked and kneeling with her ankles tied together with white socks, punishment, a dirty slut for enjoying it. I am. I have to hit her some more. I have to take a nicotine break in the garden after that. Big mistake. Why didn't I just smoke it in the kitchen after my wank instead of going out to look at the sky? Cally comes home at just the wrong moment and locks up the back door, knowing I'm stuck outside. I'm excluded yet again by that gallivanting tart and made to feel guilty for it too. I try the front door instead but she's put a new chain on it and all I can get is my foot in the door and isn't that just typical? I try ramming it but she is pushing from the other side and we battle for centimetres. As I pull back my shoe to get a forceful run at it she bangs the door shut and locks it too and I am fucked and angry and outraged, and let the door have it and I don't care if all the neighbours hear. In fact I want them to hear the injustice that has been done to me, 'It is my house,' I shout, 'mine,' and I will never let her go unless I want her to. I call 999 and they are on the spot in minutes to let me in when I realise that no, actually, they are carting me away and that she has won them over with her stories and the little shit with her tales and made-up crap to get me out the house. They listen to me explaining all that as they drive the squad car and give sympathetic nods in recognition that she's a conniving cow and wasting their time. It's good to be understood. I can get out now, they say, but it's in the middle of bloody nowhere, what's the idea? To cool off, they say, and they bugger off leaving me in the Dublin Mountains twenty miles from where I began. The injustice of it all. I hate her even more for this. I've got less than I started off with. At least this morning I had a roof over my head and that briefly improved to being my own roof. Now I've none and it's really cold. The rain has long since hardened to ice. I've no idea where I am in the dark countryside or which way to walk to get out of it, despite my Scouting in the seventies. Follow the road? Back then we would go orienteering with at least a torch, a compass and the Ordnance Survey to guide us over Wicklow at night. And Toby. He always knew how to do the map reading stuff and we'd keep in tight behind him, trusting he'd head us in the right direction and get us all to base camp for a feed and a feel when we stuffed our wet socks down each other's jocks and laughed at the boners and at those who couldn't get it up. He got us there and got us home. Always finding our way. All places leading to all places.

There are noises away to my left and the way of madness. They persist and so do I. Maybe it is the sound of sheep but they don't bleat at night. I quicken my pace to get ahead of them, hoping I am going forward and not around in circles like desert tourists. I can feel the difference between road surface and the crunch of frosted grass under my shoes so that keeps me on track, although my feet are getting wet from the mistakes I keep making going into the verge. My eyes are adjusting now that my heartbeat isn't pumping blindness into them. I can just about see in front of me and the fear edges away. I am developing night operative skills and I march on to keep warm, calculating if I've eaten enough to sustain me. If I carry on until morning then I could flag someone down as they head to work and I'll get a lift or get my bearings. Say I broke down and have no phone. I turn it off in case they catch me out. What is the point in having a phone for emergencies if you don't have anyone to call? I want to lob it into the darkness, get rid of my life. It's rubbish anyway. But I don't, I want to get even and that drives me on. To level the unrelenting. Cally, God, she goes on. When the kids were small she would always be nagging me to go out with them, just as the football would be coming on, always at the wrong time. She wanted us to do stuff together. Family shit, she would say, as if that's doing stuff. To shut her up I went out with her and Cassie this summer to some meadow she said would be great to roll around in and have a picnic. What for? Anyway it was just some crappy field full of barley stalks too stiff to sit on and which cut your hands and legs walking through them. We got sunburnt and covered in flies and it was a waste of time, which I knew it would be but there was no telling her.

Now the cold air is hurting the back of my lungs and I don't know if I should breathe in less to stop it and if I do will I have enough air to continue? If I dropped down dead out here no-one would know until some tractor runs me over at milking time and I've no ID and it takes two weeks searching dental records to find out who I am and by then they're all delighted because my life insurance pays out and she gets to keep the house and dances on my grave. Must cancel that policy, I won't assist her that way. Won't give her the satisfaction of me dying. I'll stop the mortgage if I can't live in it. She's a stealer of houses and pushing me to my limits. Draining my bank account for her dirty nights out on the town. She should think again of what she is losing. Money, security, it all comes from me. Do you hear me? You eat and you drink and you rabbit away, sleeping in the day time, doing nothing. You're just using our kids as the reason to stay around. You're a magpie, a home-breaker, a selfish fecking nasty lazy hormonal miserable ugly fat cantankerous useless piece of shit. Live on the dole and squirm, I'll be watching you every minute, getting poorer. You'll pay, you'll see. No one crosses me. Rights, I have. You've run out of yours. You low-life fuck-wit. Drag you by the hair and crush your face on the floor. How satisfying it would be to stamp on your head as you rant. It's your fault. You did it.

After six hours of walking it's easing a little. The volcano is shrinking, the pressure going down. It's a relief to have left some of it behind me on the byways, to have stomped and spewed a bit. At least, that is, until she annoys me again. She has invaded my brain and is frying it. She won't stop annoying me even from the other side of the mountains and I have to carry on over-ground to find a place where her probing signal can't reach me. Years of practise, she knows exactly how to get in. So I have to put up more metal mind fences to shield my defence forces while I plan vengeance, without her listening. I think quietly so that she can't hear me, of ways to put an end to her days. It is soothing, therapeutic. I watch. I wait. I plan. I come up with ideas, as best I can, on how to get my life back and get rid of hers. By daybreak I am grateful for this creative night, apart from the hell and the razor blades in my feet. I wasn't even arrested so that just goes to show…penance for nothing.

Lighter for it, I walk into town along the filling pavements, overtaking slow queues of cars. Drivers going nowhere, unaware I should be there. I'm one of them, don't you know? Morning smells and swells of people leave me feeling hungry. My wallet left in someone's home. Back to being meek and wanting, wishing I weren't and hoping for something. Oh help me Lord in this, the haunting of my life. He answers me with that yellow door. No handle on it, giving me delusions of Divinity. I'm not that far gone yet. I go round the back in search of a hot breakfast. Back to the place of the homeless freebies before the normal people took me in, Frankie that is. I just can't face the embarrassment of telling her I failed again. Not yet. I know the routine of this world and I'm glad it didn't have long enough to know mine. The duty social worker, street worker he says he's called, slides into the seat next to me. He works here a lot and was the first person I spoke to when Cally dropped me off the cliff and I didn't know where to go. I tell him I'm not stopping, just had a night outside and I'll be off to work soon.

'You can have a shower here and some warm clothes,' he offers, 'you know the ropes.'

To hang from.

He doesn't believe me, that I have a decent life, a job to go to. Even though I haven't managed to get there for a while. I look down and yes, I could do with a change after that hike. He sits in silence the way we do and I tell him I want to get back into my house, that I went last night but got caught out and can he lend me some money to try again today? He tells me to swing by the office so he can write out a travel credit and when we're in there our chat returns to why I left home in the first place. He had it written out the first day I came to the hostel, so I don't know why he has to go through it again.

'You mentioned your daughters and your wife's reaction to the news that led you to here...'

'No that's all cleared up now. Andi, my daughter, knows it was nothing, it was just a confusion.'

'A confusion?'

'Yes, that's all. She came in last night with my youngest.'

'She came here, to see you?'

'A cafe, yeah. All sorted. I'm moving back in when I can get the locks changed. Wife's on a wobbler but she'll come round once we can sit down and talk like adults.'

'I see,' he says.

Always the understanding one. There is nothing he hasn't heard, he says, and it's true I've seen some of the serious head cases he has to look after in here, who don't want looking after at all they just want to jack up or to drink up and they just tell him to fuck off. I wonder why he does it as a job.

'Everybody needs someone,' he says, 'you're not here to be judged, just to be helped. Because you never know one day the little bit of help we give will be the big bit of help that someone needs to be themselves again, or to be safe.'

'Sounds like a vocation to me. Without the altar boys,' but he doesn't laugh so I make my excuses and go upstairs to get cleaned up and Christ my feet are killing me. The shower is weak and barely warm but I want to stay in here instead of stepping out onto the cold lino smelling of portaloos and back into a life gone so transient and shit I don't recognise it's mine. I want to give it back. Crying on my own and hoping the steam and shampoo will cover it up in case anyone cared enough to look, which they don't. Dog-eat-dog in here. Nothing left for Blackie to bury. Only for the street-worker guy but he's paid to be nice so no one else has to. And he writes us all down and files us away in a locker room to be forgotten. It's alright, he says, it's the start of a brand-new day. The homelessness would be alright if it weren't for all the other homeless people watching me falling. Fallen already. But never as badly as them. I'm not in limbo for an infinite number of years. Once I get back into the house everything is fixable. This is a small diversion into DIY, a glitch in my marriage and we'll look back in years to come and wonder how we were so stupid that it came to this. I text Cally asking her to come collect me, I love her.

But I am answered by some fella walking in and handing me an envelope saying,

'You have just been served notice,' and he walks off. How did she do that? It's a court paper, something about no contact with the family and dates and threatening stuff. I don't understand the legal jargon, just that the meaning is mean and intended to seem oh so scary. I take it to the street-worker to explain it to me. I wish I hadn't. I don't think he understands, but he says it's very clear. I cannot go home, I cannot be with my kids.

'It's a mistake,' I tell him.

'You'll have your chance to explain on the tenth. You have to be in the family court then for a hearing. Don't miss it.'

'I'll be back home by then. Cally will explain everything.'

'No. This bars you from entering the family home. You return there and you can get locked up for it.'

'This is all very confusing. How did a court get involved in a stupid family argument that is already sorted?'

'This order was granted this morning, meaning your wife was in court this morning and applied for a Protection Order, which the Judge granted. These things are normally temporary until a full hearing, that's on the tenth, when the court will decide how to proceed. You need to get a solicitor before then.'

'A solicitor? I don't need a solicitor. I don't want to get divorced or anything. I just want to go home. It's my right.'

'Well, not yet it isn't. Don't mess things up for yourself, will you? I'm telling you, this is very clear that you mustn't go back home, yet. We can help guide you through this, while you mind yourself.'

'But I've nowhere to stay,' and his head veers around the place meaning I gotta stay here again and that is just shit. It's just not fair. Why is she crushing me? Applied for protection from what? And not answering my texts? What twisted story has she invented now?

'Meanwhile…' and he goes on about ways he can do this that and the other and none of them include what I need him to do which is to sort out this mess caused by a bundle of lies.

Instead he fills my days with cooking and art classes and drippy pop on the radio until I can't stand the smell of boiled cabbage anymore. I head out and jump the train to the seafront just like we used to when out for the day in Skerries, crab-dipping off the pier with chips for bait. I walk across the tracks in the soft rain. The food kiosks are battened down, the big hotel boarded-up for more than a season. It's ballroom blackened by arsonists and a carpark grassing over. Decayed couples walk their dogs slowly. Not helping, walking past lives. And the air lands feebly on the promenade. The aquarium is the only thing open. €12.50 to look at fish. I follow a group of pensioners inside and skip the fare as they confuse the concierge with their confusion. I stay back in the darkness, passing vast glassyness. Stingrays. Mostly stingrays. Must be easy to catch. Sinister outlines and inane grins. Underside, they just look dim. Next are the Toxic Terrors for dragging you into deep waters. I stare into the memories of fish in other places. An enormous Sea Park me and Toby went to while visiting our brother Peter in Canada. It was in the basement of a vast and overheated mall, with a full-sized ship protruding up through the galleries. For what? That and it's sea creatures marooned two days away from the ocean. Three brothers, all looking into the deep marine pool. I felt an overwhelming sense of something and wrapped my arm around Toby's broad shoulder. He let me keep it there as I pulled into him. He didn't move, legs pressed apart, grounded and firm. I breathed into him and he followed with a breath out, pushing into the salty railings. Peter slapped me on the back and it was over, but it was long enough to remember and want more. But the dynamic was changed. Peter, excluded or disgusted, rushed us out of the place and the magic was gone.

The pensioners are spilling around me. One of them asks where she can tickle the plaice. I don't know, so she engages me about the practise. For too long. I want to go back there, to my moment, but she is invading my personal space with her need to speak. Why the fuck won't she leave me alone? She rabbits me up against the wall until her friend Ivy removes her as their group passes and apologies from old people right in my face. I escape through the exit.

Back at the shelter I find myself sitting in an AA meeting full of down-and-outs. I'm not like them. I am Brian Ferry singing about their 'Street Life.' I shouldn't be in here. Caused by a grudge of hers against me. I don't have a drinking problem, I say, haven't I been here all this time without one drink and don't feel the need for one at all? I can take it or leave it, me. No-one's forcing me to be here, they say. Vindicated by a bunch of alcoholics. One step at a time.

They give us pocket money to live on and soup kitchen dinners. Plenty of food when you're too hungry to eat it. And I have to stand in that queue to be shamed, to be waiting. A public display of our downfalls. Why not just put us in stocks and be done with it? I have money, you know, just not the access. I need proof and that's at home. I'll get on to it. There's an internet café where I start on the process of rebuilding the finances. Success. The transfer of funds and closing of policies, directing to mail boxes and change of addresses. The admin of moving my life. Sixty thousand euro I see sliding out from under her, wanderer that she is. No pleasure until she knows it. I can't resist the email, telling her that she's blown it. I'm a wanking banking impresario. Reasons to be cheerful. Stage one. Sick note into work guilt-tripping HR Christine. Now she'll put my wages and pay-outs into newly formed savings. So big and so new and so pristine. Stage two. Not to be stupid. Stage three. Enjoy it, it's for me.

Cally

It's my second time in the family courts. Knowing the geography of the building but I still have no idea when or where to go and I can't understand the tannoy announcements over the din of people in the foyer. Railway station fear of missing the train. So many people and no-one telling anyone anything. Looking for a solicitor who is in here somewhere for me. Panic over that. There are platforms full of briefcases, abandoned by legal people jostling in confident bunches. Other crowds with their supporter clubs, and I have no-one. Normally it would be the man I am here to stop. I spot him sitting on a bench with some woman and a besuited legal who got the case and the case standing over him. They see me. I hide behind pillars. I want to go home. I don't want to do this, me against him. He stares through the serious architecture, boring holes through my confidence. My nerves are melting, I'm ready to scream. I was told it would be held in camera as in no cameras allowed, it's private and there is nothing private about this public exposure. Names being called, people standing, the shaming and embarrassment. I overhear solicitors speaking from their special places, asking clients what they are here for. Divorce, separation, mostly for not paying maintenance, so I am in the right building. It's an auction, a market place for trading places. One marriage hell-hole into another. Resting now as I listen to their personal circumstances. Eight years one woman says she has been coming in here and still no money off her ex and her son nearly grown up now and it'll be too late. What is the point all the mothers ask themselves, while the dads smile in smug relief, and the kids get eff all while the legals buy a holiday home in Turkey. My representative finds me, gives me orders. I feel like an idiot. I sweat, I shake, my hands are cold. She has the look of a Jackie about her and that assured Anglo Irish voice of authority, superiority. She doesn't even need to dress-up to look the part. You can see it in her understated hair and mary-jane shoes. Louis is eyeing up the Loreto girls wearing their showy, expensive, tight skirts and black stilettos, still teetering to gain some height in their race for supremacy, ascendency, a different class.

A face appears and says,

'I'm here to support Louis.'

'What? Fuck off.'

'I thought you should know.'

Deaf is she?

'Fuck off,' I repeat for her, slowly and clearly. She does.

'Who was that?' asks my Legal.

'Don't know, but she sounds like the one he got pregnant years ago, Frankie, when he was busy with all the kids down the alleys thing.'

We both raise our eyebrows at the cesspool overflowing.

She reckons he's amoral. So he'll still get into Heaven, the Holy Shit. And all the while something is grilling down inside of me, about the pointlessness of being here. She talks, she questions and re-questions me and I'm losing all connections. Oh God, how will I cope?

'Only pyrrhic victories in here,' she says.

And I know that, I tell her, the Greeks and the Romans. She thinks I don't, but I do.

There's an inaudible announcement, then silence. My name is announced. My name, my name! A rush of everyone pouring around me, leaving me, leading me, follow me, someone says. Into a court like lemmings, sheep, wives, all of us to the slaughter. I want to die, to fall, nothing at all when we are told to rise when the Judge comes in. Stuck in the cage, too late to leave. No talking please. Was I talking to myself? See Louis there in the middle row. Wanting to ask his advice. Christ. The time it takes. My Jackie bobs up and down a few times, like her hair, sparring with the others and putting them in their place. Glad to have her on-side, rather than against. She is talking to the Judge, I shake, standing up for inspection. The terror draws down, it's hard to hear or see. Themis and her blindness. See me swear on Bibles. The judge is talking and walking all over me and I have to tell him about the Momentous Event and I chuck in the bit about the one waiting outside who he got pregnant at fifteen, ask her if you like, and my Legal butts in saying,

'Hostile witness,'

God what a family tree and the Judge turns to me again and I tell him just how hostile she was to me now and…

'That's all,' he commands.

Louis is up next with his faux oaths and his show-time suit, not its first performance. He'll believe him. His turn for The Biggest Story Ever Told. He won't look up. In case he turns to stone. Snakes everywhere.

'Mr Louis Loughlin.'

I'm sinking.

He makes up some saga blaming it all on history. When Judge asks him to clarify he says it's so complicated and he can't even remember his own trilogies. That's the trouble with lies, they never stand up under questioning. He gives several different versions and Judge is getting bothered and reading out stuff from years ago. Then recent reports, schools, social workers, hostels, a huge long feed of words and hearts bleed and where was he staying? Was Louis determined, aye he was that alright, to return to the family home? Could he explain that, Judge wants to know?

I want to know.

'It was a very confusing time, you have to understand,'

Louis says.

Judge rants back, having a very difficult time trying to do exactly that. Wants explanations. He goes looking for them in lists of paperwork and loses me, the relevance to the ending of our relationship. Louis claims it was just a misunderstanding.

You can't pluck lies from a Promethean, without them growing back. More gack.

'Family Court, my arse,' Louis mutters quietly.

His Legal ignores him and goes on about extenuating circumstances and drinking and Louis is very nearly arguing with that too. And then they are all on about head reports, about Louis, adjournments, dates, is that alright? I'd say if it was, if I knew what it meant. Asks if we're seeking a legal something or other and he's on about the kids. Roundabouts until we are dismissed. Louis will go mental over that. And the rest, if he knew what it meant. If I did. They don't know, they won't be the ones getting it. And then I get it all over again when the Judge calls me back for more of it. But instead he is telling me where to go for support services and did I hear him clearly, am I listening, he asks? He's right, I find it very hard to do with all this going on, I'm missing what's going on. He writes something on a scrap of paper and leans down over his podium to hand it to me, says I need it. I do. I need his kindness even more. A parachute opens. And it didn't even happen to me, a little voice says in my head. Don't look back, it did, says another.

Outside, Louis is waiting for Frankie. He was quick enough to get back in there. Christ he is walking over to me, leaning in, confiding about today's proceedings. He even feels indignant. The hypocrisy, the feel sorry for me, as he edges closer and chances are he'll turn on me. Why is he even talking? I keep it light, polite, but he's annoying me. Sidling in to make me see. Make me be. Nothing. Him and his carry-ons, pushing-in on me. Minotaur eyes.

Andi

I get Mum's version of Judge Rinder. Scary. It was too, she says. Like, who cares? Says she is doing it for me. Really?

'He has rights,' she tells me, ignoring mine, 'so he can carry on however he likes, even if he is too drunk to notice. Mind you, they said he's off it now.'

'He's never too drunk to not know what he's doing. And he's still a shit without it.'

'True. But still, what do you want, do you want to see him?'

I can't believe she just asked me that. Seriously? I hate them both for pretending.

'But he is still your Dad and loyalties and, well, at least I'm doing something now. Better late than never.'

Always late. Too late.

She talks about supervision, worst case scenario, choices being made for me, adult dilemmas. Mine. Me seeing him,

him seeing me.

'A parade charade,' is what she calls it, 'worst case scenario.'

For who, you? She is all about herself, all about her and Dad. I wish she would just sit and watch About The House like everyone else's mother on a Tuesday night and give me instalments instead. Not the ick about them but WHAT IS HAPPENING? Why can't she just answer that? Have I joined the My Parents Are Getting Divorced Club yet? Are we going to spend alternate week-ends carting Adidas bags across town on the Luas like half my year and use that as an excuse for forgetting Maths home-work?

'I left it at my Dad's.'

'Where exactly is that?'

'Balbriggan.'

'Well, what do you expect.'

Broken homes, no formulas.

Geraldine in my class says her Dad lets her do anything now that her parents have split up. And her Mum gives out yards so you mustn't let on, she says. No difference. Cassie knows there is something different. She is different and I don't just mean her normal weirdness. She is super-fucking mental weird now, although Mum reckons she's better without him around to scare the bejesus out of her. She scares the bejesus out of me sometimes. She mostly sleeps in a tent at the bottom of my bed, made of blankets. Smells mank. Her sailing boat, she calls it, for escaping from islands in the sea. Or escaping the sea. Or whatever, just go along with it, if it makes her happy.

'Good morning Salty Seadog,' I whisper through her sails when she's snoring.

'I'm still Blackie.'

'Don't get seasick in there.'

Crap, now she is wide-awake and standing on deck, scrubbing the decking. She wants to know why Mum was getting all dressed-up really early yesterday, before sunrise. Before captain's orders.

'She even put make-up on. Is she ill?'

You could say that. You could say a lot, but I don't. Not to her. I'm no school shrink but they always answer a question with another question,

'Why do you think that?' I ask her. Smart.

'I don't know. When I watched her she looked sad until she coloured her face in.'

'Do you watch her a lot?'

'I am the look-out. I see she will be happy if Daddy comes home. From my crows-nest at the top of my ship pole.'

'Mind you don't fall out,' cue to fall out. She does. Mock agonies on Atlantic Homewares carpet. We roll in waves across oceans and onto the landing. Mum is standing. There. Up early two days in a row. No wonder Cassie is worried.

Cassie

When I tell Mammy that we'd gone to see Daddy that time and he is coming home forever soon she goes all stiff-faced so I know she has heard me but she pretends she hasn't and then she shouts at Andi a lot who says it's my fault. They are both pulling my new emoji jumper, playing tug-of-war, but playing mean like the face at the bottom with cross eyebrows. All of the faces are getting twisted up and angry and…

'I just want my jumper back! I just want my Daddy back!'

'No you don't.'

But I do. Because it's weird without him. Because it's nice without him. Because I don't know what it is without him. That's all. I become Blackie who knows how to do this sort of thing and I jump up and grab my jumper with my teeth.

'Christ, look what you've done to her,' Andi shouts and jumps back.

And Mammy doesn't say anything again because she never does and I go outside and take myself for a walk. I meet Mrs Snail, that's what we call her, and she says, 'hello,' nicely and pats me on the head and I follow her for a bit, getting that old lady smell, but she tells me to stand up or my knees will get sore. They are not sore but now I have to sit on the grass and wait until I am a grown up and can do what I like and tell children to do what they don't like doing. I watch Mrs Snail disappear around the corner towards her cottage on the other side, with her bag on wheels. Once she told me she keeps dead babies in it and to stop asking so many questions. I suppose that's why she lives on her own, because she killed all of her babies walking home from the shops with them so slowly. And she has to keep going back for more, but the same thing happens. I could offer to pull her bag for her. It would be a lot quicker but I don't want to in case I see inside it or I get asked inside her house. I don't actually want to play with her. She lives in the blue door with plastic flowers outside that Andi doesn't like. I like them because they are always there for Mrs Snail so that she doesn't forget where she lives if she sees another blue door and gets confused. But all of our doors are grey anyway. Everyone gets new paint from Aldi to make their door look different so they all look pavement-coloured. Only old people paint their doors blue. If I had my own door I would have emojis on it so people would smile and want to come in. Me and Mammy like emojis too much, Andi says, and that you can tell Mammy is old too and has just discovered them because she sent a cat emoji to Tesco Mobile because she said they would like it. Blackie could be an emoji but they haven't invented that one yet on Andi's phone. She lets me play on it sometimes but gets annoyed when I do and then forgets and lets me have another go. I keep looking for a Blackie. There is a ginger emoji dog but I don't like it. It reminds me of the little dogs we saw running in circles around their dead mammy on the road after our car just hit it. All the cars stopped because they didn't want to run over any more puppies and Mammy said it wasn't her but it was. I heard it bang and pop open under our car. That's what it sounds like when you die. Then a big crow bird hopped over when the grownups were shouting at each other through their car windows and it scared off the running-around-puppies because it wanted to see if the dead dog would wake up. When I was little we had a small white dog called Jack for three weeks. He had to go and live with a man in a big garden because he couldn't stop messing in our house and Mammy said she always knew he would. He was so fun. She should have played with him more, then she would have kept him. Like my Daddy. Did he poo on the floor? Maybe I didn't play with him enough? Mammy comes out and gives-out to me for going outside without telling her.

'I never have to tell you,' I say.

'Well you should. You should tell me where you are at

all times. Anything could happen to you and I wouldn't know where you are.'

'But I'm always here. Outside.'

'You have to tell me now. It's a safety rule.'

She has new rules. Loads of them. But she forgets them, and me. And they are mostly about making play boring or about me having to tell her stuff that I don't know what it is she wants me to say. Like the lady we went to see who weighed me then said she wanted to play with me but she was useless at it and kept asking how to play with the dolls until I showed her and she kept getting bored and writing stuff until I said I could write too and she let me use the colouring table while she asked me questions I couldn't answer. She asked me if I was worried about anything and I told her I was, that Andi is going to die, like ants and stars. She said that's never going to happen, at least not for a very, very long time. So I felt stupid then because stars are forever. She said,

'That was fun,' but it wasn't and, 'will you come again?' and I didn't want to but you have to say yes to grownups.

Later Andi said she had to speak to the weird lady too, but that it's okay, she was only trying to help. She wasn't.

'She needs help, she doesn't know how to play,' I have to go back to teach her and I'll miss school for a good reason, said Mammy. When I am older I will understand. I am going to be six on my next birthday and then I will know everything.

'Can I have a party Mammy?'

That is the worst thing in the world I could have asked for. Mammy cries. Andi is really nice to me so we go to her room and she wears her other butterfly wings. We both dress up and play fairies on her bed. She is awesome. We are best friends.

'No, you are my little sister,' she ruins it so I leave.

Mammy is cleaning the house again. She keeps doing it again and again, even though it is really clean and tidy now. She has just learnt how to do it and can't stop, like when I got my new Flicker. I couldn't ride it at first but when I worked out how to make it move forward by wobbling my bum side-to-side I stayed on it all the time, even when it got dark. Even before it gets dark and then when it does get dark Mammy bleaches everything in the house because she says it's still dirty and her bum goes side-to-side too when her arm rubs the floors and cupboards and shelves and all of the handles that she says he touched.

'He touched me and I'm not still dirty,' I say, and she rushes me into the bath and fills it with Dettol and cries because she says it stings her eyes. I cry too but that's because Dettol smells like a sick bucket.

'Don't tell anyone that. It's not nice,' she says.

'No. I'm not sure which bit isn't nice.'

'All of it. All those anniversaries.'

'What's any verses?'

'Too many mistakes.'

'Me?'

'No of course not. You were never a mistake. We always

wanted you.'

'Daddy doesn't want me now though.'

'He does. He just can't have you, that's all.'

'Why not?'

'Not all grownups are good at being parents.'

'Are you?'

'What do you think?'

And I think about it and she is being really good right now, apart from the always cleaning thing and her new rules, but she forgets them. So I say,

'Today you are a very good parent,' and she smiles and cries even more so I stop talking and lick her hand instead. She washes the taps.

'Those aren't dirty. They actually live in the bath,' I say.

'They have actual invisible bacteria on them.'

'They found bacteria on Mars.'

'Filthy stuff, gets everywhere.'

'Mrs Snail kills the ones on her plastic flowers with a steam cleaner. She got it in Argos for 89.99.'

'They have intergalactic super cleaning powers.'

'So do you.'

'Not enough.'

And she re-does the loo.

Toby

I've been going round Cally's house since Louis was chucked out. Doing odd jobs, checking up on them. For his sake, letting him know what they're up to. Not that they get up to much, apart from that one night of madness when Cally thought she was seventeen again and Andi wished she was too. Mid-life crisis and the mid-teens, doing pretty much the same thing while their friends all hate each other by 'liking' their comments online. I just like to look, but on-screen. Had to load some spy app onto her phone for Louis the other day, wants to keep track of her. I don't mind but there are limits, the boring shite she comes up with. Who would want more of it? It's a back-to-back commentary on her very own series of Obsessive Compulsive Cleaners, without ever getting to the finale where they realise the extent of their condition and drag the Hoover off into semi-retirement. Making up for lost time, I reckon. Their house was always a kip. She says she's cleaning up the lost time. Head-case. The rest of the time she's just Googling Jamie Oliver recipes which she never cooks or watching back episodes of Homeland over and over again. Just watch the news woman, there is a world out there with foreign politics and it's not all about you. If she and my brother just showed some initiative in travelling beyond their family breakdown to some other place, do things differently and the same, get a life beyond their monotony of small-minded revenge and sort things out. Their unit holds the rest of us in place. If Louis is not careful he'll end up a permanent feature of Dublin's streets, shooting off like Bang Bang. No one's smiling at Louis. He really has to drop it and find some purpose. I was aimless too when I first separated, wandering abroad visiting relatives. Their stability only highlighted the lack of mine and pointed to my pointless future. I just didn't know my mind. I needed to go looking for it. Louis dragged along, thought he was homesick for the family he had left behind, despite the rake of siblings we visited. He'd be too scared for such an adventure now, of what he'd find. Of saying hello to a new life of rum and Copacabana. Not forgetting the Zika midgets. The website says that, if infected, it can be spread through intercourse. Like some giant mosquito dick of death and deformity from Bible times, but not so polite. Mossie repellent versus the Fourth Horseman of the Apocalypse. I was telling Andi about it all but she was only interested in whether or not they have Snapchat in South

America, like that's the second most important thing at the end of the World. I told her Putin will get us all before the flies do but she thought I meant puking and really she's just a kid. Her dad is too, so I'm not holding my breath there. To give him space, or to slap him across the face and tell him to wake up? The dilemma of dealing with brothers. I am drawn to and away from him in equal measure. I need to sever his umbilicus our mother glued to me when she was too busy having babies of her own every year so the priest would send her to heaven. It was much easier to yank them out once they'd cut her pelvis in half. Why stop when God invented symphysiotomies? There is always a reason to escape. There is always an escape and a way back in. But Louis is extremely hard to track down right now. Phone off and not in work, not like him to be mysterious. He only calls when he needs something, short and quick with the excuse that he is either borrowing a phone or there are restrictions on its use or such crap. He's in a right flap, blowing his life away, waiting for me to tether him back to it. I could just leave him to fall off the edge while I have the chance, a fitting end to a dangly life. And there it is again, our invisible cord. I can get rid of him but I can never get rid of him. I try contacting by email to meet up. It could be days before the dope visits an internet cafe to read it, if those places still exist. Or have they gone the way of libraries, laundries and video rentals? I saw an outdoor launderette in a garage forecourt recently. Talk about being forced to wash your dirties in public. A drive-by scandal, it is. But I'm not giving up on my auld sinner Louis, as he drags himself away from his wife and kids.

Then out of the ether my brother replies from his technical desert,

'See you tonight in Madigan's?' he writes.

Louis

The barman serves six people, I'm counting, before taking my order. I was first, I could take offence. And them being tourists.

'The usual?' he asks.

I don't have one. He goes for the Carlsberg anyway.

'Guinness doing well?' I nod in the direction of the visitors.

'Stag. It'll be a good night.'

For someone.

A silent game is on the big screen. Can't see the score. I'm even losing track of which match and where Arsenal's at. What are you fucking supporting them for? Toby will say when he comes in the door. Our starting point for starting all our wars again. I didn't deliberately pick them. It came right out of thin air when I was seven and he had me in a Nelson and I'd run out of good expletives and contradictions to his torments,

'Up for Arsenal!' I shouted and it's stuck with me ever since, my arsenal of Arsenal to beat my brother with. He tied me to our back gate with Man U scarves for that. So I yelled down the alleys for London, until enough people wanted to thump my head in and I got hauled inside for being an embarrassment. It pays to sing when you're a young one. Unless you're Cassie. She just nicks everything to bury in her mud heaps littering the lawn. 'My life,' I want to shout, 'you took that and stuck it where no one could find it,' I may have said that out loud. The tourists are looking.

'Local character,' barman apologises.

I very nearly bleeding well am.

Toby arrives at half time. Knows the score already. At least some of it. He doesn't know that I've been staying at Frankie's house on and off, mostly since the family court case.

'How did you get back in there?' he asks. Then, realising the stupidity of the question, 'not for the first time.'

'I'm on the sofa. She's an ex. Or should I say ex ex? And the daughter.'

'Isn't she very good to you all the same? All these years?'

'Aren't I very good to them you mean,' sure, they feed me and all that. Haven't we made up for our measly Friday night meetings over the years when everything was undercover and I had to sneak in for a couple of hours on my way home and pretend to Cally that I was getting a takeaway for the end of the week or having a couple of drinks with the lads and that would explain the cash they managed to get off me each time with their sob stories and, 'needing a man about the place,' and, 'aren't we first in your life,' and all that goes with implying the threat that they might tell if I didn't give it to them, but it was never spelt out like that and so now they are paying me back. Things have a way of working out.

'Better than staying in that old hostel,' Toby says.

'Keep your voice down, I don't want everyone to hear I was in there,' I warn him. They didn't, their lives are too noisy to hear mine. Only Frankie would have heard his broadcast, back in her kitchen, listened to me and helped. Shame Toby wasn't so generous voicing information years ago when she got up the duff.

'Why didn't you tell me about Frankie when she got pregnant?' I ask him.

He feigns bewilderment, sees I mean it, catches up,

'Louis, everyone guessed. Assumed you did too. You were young, life went on, that's just how things worked back then'

'I still looked out for them, when I knew.'

'Can't think why. The kid could have been anyone's. You'd get a DNA test these days.'

'Nope. She has the look of me.'

'That was no reason to let it plague your life. Her family had it all sorted until your duty interfered.'

'She wasn't an interference,' like yours was, I want to say. I was still young the day our parents locked-down the parlour over his. Always a sign of a serious misdemeanour. Regular every-day rollickings rolled out our mother's mouth on a ten minute kitchen basis, but a lashing required best furniture. The rest of us checking out who was missing from the hallway, the pleasure of someone else's punishment. Only low talking. Our sister Janet summoned in. No one getting a belt. Fecking serious. Conversations finished, us scarpering. Guessing and waiting to be filled-in. Only years later did the taunts make sense, why our older sister emigrated, doing a Frankie.

'But I could have been with Frankie all these years instead of humping harping Cally,' I complain to Toby.

'They're all the same, Frankie, Cally, whoever. It's not like you were mad about each other.'

He's right. It's not like I even knew her that well either. I just knew I had to parade a girl, be seen to be doing a line, stop the rumours that I was into back street passages of a different kind. Definitions being important at that age. Frankie obliged. She obliged a bit too much sometimes and was fond of a congratulatory audience to prove that she was 'doing it.' It just meant that I had to, you know, perform to order. Nothing new about that. I genuinely didn't know she got pregnant. Bet there was no applause for her then. She just stopped coming round. Her Mam frowned the next time I called. She slammed the door in my race to escape when she said her Frankie had, 'gone away for a rest,' and I spent the next six months relieved I wouldn't have to do her again. When I saw her pushing a babbie in town I just thought what a slut, typical, girls like that, you can't marry them. And that's when she told me it was mine. In God's Holy name, Jesus, you don't deliver news like that outside of Arnotts. Unbelievable. I told her, I did, I was seeing Calypso Wainright.

'That effing jumped-up tart!' she cried, 'who the eff does she think she is with a name like that?'

'Cally, we call her.'

'We? Tis far from where she was reared.'

I didn't know which offended her more, the name or her status as my new girlfriend. It was definitely the name, I'd decided, because I ended up reassuring her that it would soon be changed to mine. And there, I'd gone and proposed without even asking my future wife. Before I even got home our Mam had the news, the church booked and her hat redesigned for the wedding. I never really did ask Cally, although she swears I did. Too pissed, she was, and eager to stop me living. That worked then.

Toby slaps the bar for another drink, while charming the staff with one of his winks. His stance planted and powerful. Dressed for the part. How does he do that? Why am I always the gimp in the tartan trousers and the acrylic hair? He has that look about him of a pioneer fur trapper from some Hudson Bay Company outpost. Check shirt, not quite a handlebar moustache. Nothing like The Village People. All he needs is the rifle over his shoulder and some leather chaps. Him the frontiersman, and I am not dressed to play. Mountain of a man. Some folks are meant to be one. He catches me staring and feeds me another pint, just like any other night. Every night that we spend together, re-enacting ancient battles. A woman pushes between Toby and counter. I watch him count-down for round one. Still proving himself to me. He mock-pulls her back onto his lap as he grabs a stool for a prop just to stop. The fall that was never going to happen. He buys her a drink by way of apology. Then another. He is showing me. With his back to me. Like he always does. He'll take her to his room, leave me to finish the chasers. I pre-empt their departure by asking for a rum. No, a bottle of it. Pay upfront. They stay for that, alright. As she drinks from it, her mouth burns and we imagine what we both want to do to soothe her open face. She even drips some down her front, on purpose to make us stare. The liquid seeps down her bare cleavage. Toby swipes my hand away for wiping it off.

'What, are you twelve?' he shouts as I lick my fingers, embarrassed and twelve. And twenty-five and thirty-five and retirement age. She sneers and talks about leaving. I sneer and think about relieving myself. Over her. Toby pushes my arm, says I'm harmless, hitting me too hard. Stand there and take it. Festering slowly. The two of them move away, thanks be to God, to the back room where the tourists are dancing two hours too early and it's getting jammers in here for a week night. I could almost be in Foleys, except there's 'no mauling allowed.' Should have put a sign up. I'm rumming it down, encased in the dense scrabble to give orders. Watching the squeeze thicken. Blood loosen.

Refill the glass. I'm nearing the bottom. Nearing maudlin when Toby reappears to finish the bottle and drags me away to the salsa night inside. Says it's full of women, as well as that one Katarina, she's called. He pulls me through the dark tunnel where Latin music channels from the rear room. It's noisy and tight. People. Smelling the Spanish as they raise their arms and spill in erotic sways, in and out of each other. A Mexican wave pours towards me, so fast I lift and dance and Toby's head laughs and it's nothing like the diddly dee of our schooldays when we held ourselves flat, only moving from the knees down lest the Devil heard our tunes and we might actually enjoy it. If I had Uncle Brown's Irish dancing skirt on now, that would do it. Knee-high socks. Rocks. And I'm back. Stop it now. I sidle and grind to everyone's beat. The heat is something else in here. Toby swings by me, swaps partners, slips a hand around me and I'm bound in his spell. He breaks it. By slapping against my wet shirt.

'My sweat,' I exclaim. Except that he is sweatier than me and we stop in our places, creating an obstruction and steaming. Humidity pours over us both, draping us and dripping off onto the warm parquet, rum-flavoured and dank. Walls close in. His woman interrupts, the perfect solution to air pressure. Or not. They dance away, flaunting it, rubbing it in. I watch the traitor. Them. I can't stay. With it, with him. Hunting for a boy that I can't have. He's my brother, for Christ's sake. And now he's at my back, following me outside. Just the two of us walking home together to

Frankie's. No need to confront a brother. Who smothers pasts. He knocks on Frankie's door, for ages. Eventually she wakes and lets us in. And we have her. At fifteen. She knows him after all these years. Didn't everybody know her? She is pissed at me for being pissed. We only want to sleep. On a chair, anywhere will do, just not with you. She gnashes away to bed and we stretch out downstairs, him on the sofa, me on the floor. I am only playing on my phone, trying to wind down when Toby leaps over and grabs it off me.

'Filthy little fucker,' he calls me, just for being in some chat room asking for a video call. He reads it out. So then it opens live webcam and I have to like scrap with him to get it back, the bastard. We are up on the sofa fighting and he has my wrists and he's listening to this kid talking, making a right show of me he is, all live. The phone drops and he's asking what's it all about. Obvious. And he reckons she is half alright herself, grabbing a look. I'm astride him shouting when Frankie stamps the ceiling and I get thrown off. I grab the phone and turn it off.

'You're patient, I'll give you that,' he says, 'all that drivel would do my head in.'

'You won't tell, will you?'

'Who would I tell? No harm done. Just a bit of fun.'

I roll over. We are more alike than he thinks, I just wish we weren't. He is good at selling us, at making-up, at covering-up. Such persuasion, to forget things. He is convincing as we're inching, slowly across the floor. Pecking order restored and the years put between us divide us some more.

'Sorry,' I say, to his sleep. Sorry for being me. Saying
sorry on the day we got caught in the alley. Young
Maurice running out past Mrs Riley. Screaming, he
was, as he ran off and she hauled us in as examples
of a terrible wicked sin. Me and Toby, she'd decided.
Words were said. Then our Ma made us go round and
apologise. To him. Like he wasn't enjoying himself.
The gang got wind of it and followed us, keen for
a spectacle on a boring summer afternoon. Then
his Ma goes and answers the door and we weren't
expecting that and Toby went all tongue-tied. Never
been like that since.

'Well?' she asked, like she already knew, and
yelled for Maurice to come downstairs. His eyes were
all red and teary and we were saved by his show of
embarrassment. We even had the audience.

'It's about the alley,' Toby began, boys tittered,
'when it was your Maurice's turn,' an explosion.

And he was further interrupted by the weasel's
feeble pleading, pulling the back off his mam. She
slapped him and the chorus cheered and she said she'd
get them too, the dirty little feckers and our crowd
just egged her on. There was no stopping them then,
giving the rise and she had the broom bashing them
and our apology was all over and forgotten. And us
the heroes. We kicked stones down the street and I
asked Toby for all the gory details of what he'd done

to Maurice. He frowned at me to stop, controlling me, the idiot savant. After all these years I still am. Still following him around.

Andi

My boyfriend is notable by his absence. Not on the roll-call. Hating the abstinence. Counting the days when he's not here. Adding them up and taking them away, hoping I'll see him, hoping he's nearby. I miss his quirks, the literature geek quoting all that stuff like it's Taylor Swift. Naff, but I try. I can't wait until I'm like him and words flow out full of confidence. He's into music. I can get into it but if I'm not careful it carefully gets really annoying, burrowing under my skin. I have to concentrate on it before it blurs into static and eats away at my nerves. It's not supposed to do that according to him. We Googled it and there's no such thing as an aversion to music. It's not a phobia because I'm not scared of it and I'm okay with all the other noises. My brain just hates it after a while and has to turn it off. He said maybe I just haven't heard the right kinds of sounds yet. So he gave me his old ipod shuffle with playlists of all these tunes. Opera. Hated it. Classical. Liked the sharp cold violin strings which cut through and cooled my synapses, but only for five minutes. 70's rock. Headbanging, to a point. Jazz. Too hard. Motown. Nothing. But they all did it, set off a bit of my brain just as I was getting into it. Maybe I'm allergic, or I heard too much of Dad's vinyl collection when I was in the womb, or they just haven't written my sort of music yet. He says everything has already been written and that we are just rearranging it like the furniture to sound new. He can spot the Parker Knolls and the GPlans, stuffed behind the IKEA rugs. He loses me sometimes, but I like that, that he's different and knows things that he shares with me. Like now, after two whole weeks of no texts or nothing and me thinking he's dumped me and then I am sure he has dumped me and I am finally getting over him when he phones as if everything is normal. It isn't normal, even to phone me, you dumped me. He didn't, he reckons, he was just sorting his head out. He loves me, he is sure of that and I am like okay, I wasn't expecting that. So we are a couple then? Except I can't ask him that. I have to go out the back, Mum is hovering.

'I love you too,' because I don't know what else to say.

'You're too young to know what love is,' he slices. I kick at one of Cassie's mounds of earth in the garden.

'Shit,' I say.

'No that's not what I meant. You do know what love is. It just hasn't been very long yet has it? Long enough for us to be tested. And we will be, and we will still love each other and be there for one another. You and me, we are meant for each other. You are my Haiku.'

'What's that?' as I spread the soil out and flatten it to create a smooth, even surface.

A short poem that doesn't rhyme.'

'That makes no sense,' as I spot a piece of sodden paper protruding through the earth.

'But it does to me, if you know the rules.'

'Teach me the rules,' and he does, but they have nothing to do with poetry. He is my guilty secret. We all have those, he says, and have to mind them carefully, otherwise we will be torn apart or our families will. If we wait then we won't have to hide what we are doing, it's nothing to be ashamed of when two people love each other. Age is just a number. I'm just like all my friends. Everybody I know has done it by now, unless they're weird or ugly and even they do it. To each other, I guess. Who's kidding who?

I lift the delicate paper out of its burial place and unwrap it to reveal a gold ring. WTF? It's too chunky to be Mum's. When did Dad take this off, I wonder?

Cally

Toby turns up just in time, he can help me out for a change. Instead he gives me his loose change, which is an insult and I say a couple of thousand more is what's needed now that his brother's left. I don't want anything, just my home and what we need to live on. That's only fair. The money's running out faster than it's coming in, what with Louis avoiding his responsibilities. You can get it off Louis when his redundancy comes, I tell him. Toby gives me a fifty for the week. For the gazillion unpaid bills which are growing in the corner and there's nothing in the food cupboard. At this rate I won't even be able to afford to get to a food bank. Always at men's mercy. I tried sorting it with Louis but can't get hold of him. Toby is silent on his whereabouts, not wanting to stir or take sides. Not wanting to believe my story of how I spend nothing on everything. And there was me standing in a queue at Aldi knowing my trolly-load cost

€58.75. That's what I'm reduced to, adding up as I go along. Should've done that with my marriage. At the check-out I squeezed luck into my card, willing my bank to cover it. Don't uncover my shame in this poverty lane of people who can't even afford Tesco. Oh God I could have died, instead I asked why the bleeding thing wasn't working.

'Try again,' in his Polish accent.

The same thing happened, 'transaction rejected,' I should've known, I only had eighteen euro and forty. Blank looks as he waited for my action and I waited for miracles to happen. They didn't. They just turned my face red.

'I'll leave it,' I said. The shopping, the pride, the insides, my head. The shite for not even offering to take a few, leave a few and re-do the counting. That would be non-efficient staff use of conveyor belt accounting. When really I was mad at the bastard who caused this by fiddling his way to our divorce list. He wouldn't see it that way, he'd just be glad that I'm starving. And who gives a shit that the kids are? Not their father. Or Social Welfare, when it comes to it. Proving his absence in a cubicle. Meanwhile the kids keep asking and I'm fed up of saying, 'no, this is what you cannot buy on the dole; shower gel, fabric conditioner, Barry's teabags, coffee-tasting coffee, breakfast rolls, Andrex,' just bin liners that burst the second your fingers penetrate the poverty of cheap loo roll dissolving, it's a commodity that lasts from Monday to Saturday and please don't do a crap after that. There's none left. And if you can afford any of the above, you're scamming the system love. You and twenty thousand others. I can tell you how many in our estate pretend they're single parents while living with their lovers. All of them. And their fellas all working too. Married to them, even, some of them. So how come the shites down the Welfare don't know that yet still manage to give me the third degree? For all their meanness and questions and officialdom being mannerly, they do eff-all about finding fraudsters down our way. It pays to be skint if you're rich. Me now, I'm down to selling the family silver. In my case it's a brown leather sofa. Seating for eating. It's a Done Deal and it's taken and it's paid for. It was a shit deal and I'm sitting on the wooden floor.

'I'm telling Louis,' said the slapper next door, when she saw it being loaded onto a lorry.

'Go fuck yourself, you'll enjoy my husband more,' and there's hers, hiding like a girl, rearing all those children. None his. And her the whore. But she's better than me now, with her wimp in tow. Because he's there. And mine isn't.

But finally, on this fine day that isn't, Toby has Louis on his phone and hands it to me knowing I need to talk to him. Beg to him.

'Where've you been Louis? I asked at the hostel, Toby, work, everyone. No one knows where you are. It's like you disappeared off the planet.'

'I was on holiday.'

I don't believe him. And then it clicks,

'With Frankie?' he was gone for well over a week. I glower at Toby for his secret brotherly pacts.

'Yeah right, Torremolinos.'

'Toby never said,' Toby makes an exit, 'what were you doing?'

'Travelled about a bit. Got some sun. You know, Dublin.'

'Isn't it well for some? Wouldn't I like to go away for the winter?'

'You can't take the kids out of the country without my permission.'

'I wasn't planning on taking any kids with me.'

'Well don't think I'll look after them. You can't go.'

You're not indispensable and you're not in control of me, is what I want to say. But he is, and he is, so I don't get to go anywhere. I want to know about this new hidden life he now has, or always had. I'm jealous, my right to possess all of his actions, thoughts and deeds. He's mine. A shit, but still he's my shit.

'We need to talk,' I say.

'About what? I've been trying to do that for weeks and you won't even answer the phone.'

'We need your help. You need to look after the girls. Money. Please.'

'You should've thought of that before you kicked me out.'

'I had to, for them. You know that.'

'For you, more like, so you could go partying like the slut you are across town, getting picked up by strangers.'

I see an opening here, it was one of his fantasies to see me doing just that. So I describe it to him, in the same way he made me talk dirty to him in bed, in my sexy voice so he knows I'm doing it for him, so he knows it isn't real. So I can get something off him.

'Do that for me then, so I can watch.'

'I will.'

'Promise?'

'I promise.'

'When? You always say that, but you never do it. Do it for me.'

'I will. I'll come and meet you in town and you can watch. Then you can pay me.'

'Perfect. Eleven o'clock, Thursday morning, at The Spire. Wear a skirt,' and I don't know if he really expects me to prostitute myself like that or not, if it's a test. If I go it's because I have to. It may be busy, 'isn't there some commemoration going on that day?'

'All the better. Celebration,' he corrects me.

And they jeer me from the other side.

'Let's be clear,' he continues, 'you are doing this, none of your moral high-jinks. I'm sending you some photos of your porn action just to remind you of how low you can go. Do you want all your friends on Facebook to enjoy them too? Everyone in your address book, family?'

'You've no such things.'

'Have a look. I'm sending them to your phone now. You can decide then whether it's worth behaving the way my wife should.'

'You can't blackmail me with revenge porn when there

isn't any.'

'Take a look at your inbox. I'll meet you down O'Connell Street.'

He hangs up, swiping me back into my place, again. There are six sordid pictures of me naked and I know how he got them. The bedroom webcams for 'home security,' he'd said. Of course he'd say that. Why should it even be a surprise? It's just one more layer on top of a thousand others pushing me down. Of me not saying 'no,' and no, I do know, 'I don't want you to be like that to me,' making me small again. I can't get those words out. I just want to splurge but I don't know how to say it all and so it just grows and grows. All those angry words flying around inside my head, acting like a magnet for all those gobshites in my life who came along and added to it. And me saying nothing at all. And things just happening to me. I'm a walk-over. One day I'll fall over from the weight of all the words wanting to fall out of me. That is the way that it goes.

Standing in O'Connell Street in the sharp winter sunshine, busy with pedestrians, we wait for each other under the clock like generations did before us. Except we aren't filled with the intense love of courting youths, just lacking youth and making a sad middle-aged effort to rekindle that spark by way of fervent degradation. Like that's going to work. But I'll make it for the money. Haven't I always? That's how it works.

'You're not going to do it are you?'

I jump as he says it from behind me, in his dirty old

man's voice. He grabs my backside and laughs and yanks me around to kiss me. An angry floundering. I pull back and he's excited by my resistance. Playing the game I smile, meek and scared the way he wants me to be, to get what I want. Bartering myself. I'm well practiced at that. He wrenches my arm to walk alongside him, fast-paced and panting he is with the sexual excitement. And me wondering where on earth this is going, can he even conform in public anymore?

'That one,' he points to an elderly pensioner sitting on a bench, 'sit next to him and chat him up. Tell him you want to suck him off.'

'No way. I can't,' in a laughter of nerves.

'Do it,' he commands.

So I sit next to the wrinkly man while Louis heads to a viewpoint forty feet away and orders me with his stare. Pedestrians flicker. I talk to the grey victim, just about the weather and the shops, what it was like down here in his father's day, and his wife who went to Heaven seven years ago, God rest her soul. Leaving an empty house too quiet and cold to keep memories warm. Jacob, he is called.

'Calypso,' I tell him and we talk about that and how she of the Greeks had her own island where she hid her lover away and he says what a story and it's all pretend, just to keep Louis thinking I'm doing it right. Jacob is delighted to be taken outside of his loneliness and I am dirtied and soiled on the inside, even though I said nothing. I say farewell and walk back over to Louis who, won't everyone notice, has his hands in his pockets. Satisfied, he tells me I did good as he takes his moist hand out to hold mine. Walking us over to the cash point machine.

'I can't believe you just did that,' his tone neither condemning nor condoning.

I await whatever comes next. He fills his wallet with notes and pushes it into my bag while steering me gently, fondly, it seems. His in mine. Slotted with time. The easy way we flow into one another.

'Come on, let's get you home,' he says and we walk on slowly with me crunching the egg-shells while his voice is full of kindly sounds. He deflates me and washes over me because isn't he so sorry for what he's done? And I'm in that comfort zone of being led by my big strong man to look after me. Not I or him, just we. Compelled.

'I'm sorry,' I say, because I always do and he nods at me approvingly before we go back to our way of being together that makes us one another and I don't even notice it happening, we're just meant to be. So easy, you see, when we're together. As he slides into place my mind stops racing because our roadmap is easy to follow. We know what to do when it's just me and him and sure didn't we hate being alone?

Unified.

His hand at the back of me, guiding me home. Opening our front door, wondering how this goes with the children. He takes over, has it under control. Knows what to say. Making things normal, hiding decay. I see Cassie skip with delight. I see, I see. Routine of everything, back in its place. Allows me to slip slowly, hiding my face. We're here for her, trying harder at being parents, at marriage, he says. Working at it for the rest of our lives, he says. Doing the right thing. Reassurance. Security. Forever. It is said.

'How are we going to tell Andi?' I ask.

'Leave that to me. They need both of us. We've already talked things over. She's good with it.'

He is soothing everything into being okay and I want him to feel wanted and I do as he says. He doesn't take advantage, he just lets me offer myself up to him when I am ready and I give him my guilt when I'm passing. For allowing our 'hiatus,' as he calls it. Makes our reunion all the more special, he says. I really must believe him when he describes how the terrible times he's just been through have changed him. Such a learning curve and he's grown from it. It took this shake-up to shake-up our marriage and to put it back on track. Don't be worrying yourself now. We have the redundancy, the savings and best of all he has a new job to go to. Yes, head-hunted, don't you know. Starts next month. Car, pension, the whole works. Convincing. Immerse.

He's playing The Average White Band, Pick up the Pieces.

Cassie

Something has happened to one of my cairns. It was the best one because it had a green foil Viscount on top. The biscuit was still inside. I saved it from school and didn't eat it because I don't like mints. I saved it specially to mark the spot. There are lots of cairns, but only one with a Viscount on top. It is all dirty now. And Daddy's ring that I buried has gone and there is mud everywhere. It was a Resurrexit. Jesus did that a long time ago and nobody could find Him and then we got Easter eggs. Perhaps He thought it was for Him. Resurrexit is also a place down the country where Mammy's cousins live. They have Holy place names there. I went there once and got given a postcard of a Holy Well. I stuck it on the fridge and Daddy stuck it in the bin. I have to build some monsters to defend the mounds, to stop everything from coming back out and running around the garden. I get some big potatoes with icky bits on them and cover them in tin foil. Then I poke the long sticks in them that we got for a barbeque and never used because we got a barbeque and it rained and now it's all rusty and fallen over. The sticks make very tall legs for my silver monster insects. They need seven each to stand up and see what is happening. They have buttons off my uniforms for eyes and an extra stick to wave around at people and look cross. I put them in-between my mounds and they start working. Blackie chases them and barks to test my army. I put Blackie in charge. They do as he says. I eat the biscuit.

Andi

Mum's been hiding in bed for days, burying her guilt under the duvet until she forgets that it's even there. And I have to carry on as normal, pretending we are one big unhappy family again. His relentless music. She bought Andrex. The cost of me.

'It was no big deal. You're making a mountain out of a molehill,' she said when I reminded her what Dad did, what he is. She says I have to 'get a grip,' as if it's my problem that I can't just move on, that I'm making a drama about it. She is operating on remote again, with Dad at the controls. He keeps on cornering me for these little chats about boundaries and family loyalties and shit and all I want to do is scream but I can't because he'd tell me to shut the feck up so I scream on the inside instead and have to cut little holes for it to come out later when I'm in my room and can lock the door so no-one sees the noise of me on my arms.

Punch it back in with a tattoo. I text the boyfriend.

Me:	want matchin tats
Him:	good idea
Me:	wen?
Him:	tonite. 5. I'll pay
Me:	deadly

We walk into this parlour he knows about and he tells the girl that he called earlier for a booking that I can have any design I like.

'Gotta have parental consent if ya under eighteen,' she says to me.

'You have it, let me speak to Dave,' he says and she slopes off back to find him. This cool guy with flowing blond hair walks out front and shakes hands with him like they're old mates, though he never mentioned him to me before. Must be in his twenties and he has the whole works done on his face, piercings and inks. Dave gets out all these design books for me to flick through and leans in over the counter as I go through them all. He is stroking the ones he's really proud of, says they'll look lovely on me, I've lovely skin. Lovely Wavy Davy, with eyes the colour of ginger sand. They're contact lenses, he says. I eventually settle on a matching pair and we agree I should go first in case I get too scared waiting. It's not as painful as I thought it would be and then it is and it's burning and stinging and I want him to stop and they are both stroking my arms telling me it's okay, just hang on in there for a bit longer and I love them doing that and hate that it's now when I can't enjoy a single bit of them feeling me up because this damn well hurts too much and tears are coming out even though I'm not crying. I bite on his sleeve, and then on his arm and they say it's like childbirth. Both pains caused by a little prick, but I don't say that because they are both so hot. When it stops I am so relieved and glad and proud, and I enjoyed the fondling when they continued on a bit afterwards, but I didn't tell them that. Then we realize the shop's already closed and moody pants at reception has already gone home so we have to leave with just my tat done and not his.

'Too bad. We'll come back again,' and they shake hands. Grown-ups.

Coming home in his car he loads a CD. Milk pours through my brain and a silky scarf pulls around it.

'What is it?' I ask.

'At Last by Etta James,' watching the relief drape over me, 'see, you just needed to find the right music to match your soul. This is about you and me.'

He's right. Until the next track, that is, and the drilling starts in my head. I turn it off.

'Oh well. Maybe there's only one song that works, because it's our love song. It's like us, we're the only ones who work together. Play it again.'

'No. It only works once. I don't want to ruin it.'

'Me neither.'

I put it back into its case. Then I remember,

'We didn't pay. For the tattoo.'

'It'll be grand.'

'We ripped them off. We won't be able to go back and get yours done. We didn't pay.'

'Well in a way I did. We have our own exchange forum, me and Dave.'

And I feel such a kid.

'What's that?'

'It's like community banking, trading. I'm in credit.'

'I do have a bank account of my own you know, for my after-school job.'

'Hey big spender,' he teases, 'but I wouldn't let you pay for anything. My treat. You're such a pleasure. I was getting real turned on in there. You were too by the looks of things. Shall we stop in somewhere?'

'I don't want to go home yet. Ever,' he looks at me questioningly, 'you haven't been round the last few days, since Dad's been home.'

'He needs his space. But I will come over more.'

'I need you there when he is,' telling him and not telling him about it for the first time.

'Why's that then?' he asks, putting his hand up my top.

'Don't,' I brush him off, showing I'm annoyed with him and persisting for the first time, 'this is serious.'

'I'm all ears.' But he isn't, only his dick is listening. Until he gets what I am actually saying about my Dad.

'Your Mum kinda told me that already. I do know.

It's okay.'

She did?

'You don't get it. He's my Dad. Isn't that illegal or something?'

'Well, you know, there's showing a little affection and then there's showing a bit too much, if you know what I mean. It all depends on what you're comfortable with.'

And I am less sure than ever about what comfortable should be. He keeps at me to get comfortable on him but I really don't want to, feeling like this, whatever this is. He takes it out and finishes himself off with me watching and I think I'm meant to be doing something, like I owe him something, for the tattoo or what, so I lean in and he accidentally on purpose pushes my head down on him and I think we are both embarrassed, but he looks pleased. He insists I go home then, so I do, needing a couple of painkillers for the top of my arm and I can't wait to take the Clingfilm off it to send pictures to everyone. Cassie tries rushing me out of the bathroom but it can't be rushed. It's called aftercare. I let her in and tell her if she's good I will tell her a very big secret, finger to the lips. She gasps in awe at my tattoo and says she wants a crow on her arm too.

'It's not a transfer. It's real.'

'Daddy will kill you,' she says, rightly.

'But he won't know will he? If he finds out I will have to kill you too. It's our secret. Just you and me.'

She likes that. Dad said he'd cry if we ever ruined ourselves by damaging the only perfect things he'd ever made. Spent all these years protecting us, he reckons, only to see us ruined by tattoos. No, he said, we're never allowed to get them. So we stay in the bathroom playing until he shouts at Cassie to go to bed, so she disappears into her ship and I pretend I'm asleep in bed too just to avoid one of his heart to hearts while Mum continues to lie down in denial. While I am not sleeping I hear Dad shouting downstairs, raging at Toby who must have come in really late and he's really giving it back some. I'm pleased Dad is getting it instead of us and I strain to listen to the words, but can't make them out. It's obvious who will win.

Louis

Toby is taking up all my living space in the living room and I want to yell at him and he asks about Andi and I've nothing to give-out about her but I want to. I confront her, like a hundred times in my head and that's how I tell her off. Usually. I might yell a bit but there's no need for a show-down, a stand-off at OK Corral. I never have arguments, me. Like that time I caught her getting off with Toby on the couch, the dirty bitch just needed a slap on the arse to stop it quick. Where my hands should be. This time she needs a darn sight more than that as I bend down to get my glass and see the screen-saver on Toby's phone. It's Andi but like an internet porn star, naked and pouring with lust, boiling the rage out of me.

'What the feck is this?' I ask him. He snatches it off me,

'She sent me a photo by mistake a few days ago. Said it was intended for her boyfriend. I've been trying to find a good time to tell you. Going by your reaction aren't I right you'd go mental? She's putting herself about.'

'What boyfriend? She doesn't have one.'

'She could have. You should know she was at me while you were away, with her flirting and sexting. You know what she's like, a sex siren.'

'No.'

'Come off it man. I've seen the way you look at her sometimes, and this whole thing with Cally chucking you out, wasn't that about something between you and Andi?'

'It was a misunderstanding.'

'Did you mistake her for an eight year old boy?'

'Don't be disgusting. I'm not one of those, you know, you know, like you.'

'Look,' says Toby, 'I'm just being honest, that's all. And you've a short memory where the boys are concerned. Look, we're an affectionate family and we'd do anything for each other, right?'

I know he's making me again.

'Yes.'

'Well then, a little kindness between relatives goes a long way and as we're all a bit, say, very kind in our family then we need to look out for each other. Andi is … amenable in that way.'

'Amenable? She's my fucking daughter, not Jenny McCauly.'

'Now you listen to me, and you listen hard,' I can see he's getting hard himself, pulling up to me, 'Andi is no innocent. She's a young woman and very gentle and sweet. I'm not having some spotty-faced skanky lad treat her like shit and get her up the spout and leave her pushing a pram full of bastards for the rest of her life. She's better than that.'

'She's my better than that.'

'She is all of our responsibility. You don't give her half enough of the affection she needs to stay at home. If you keep on ignoring her like you do, she'll go looking for it elsewhere. You have to be more physical with her, in a nice way. Treat her gently every now and again, I've been getting her used to the cuddles she should be getting from you.'

'Is that what you do?'

'Only when it suits her, if she's okay with it,' he is softening us both, pawing my arm where he was gripping it before.

'See,' he says, 'it's nice isn't it when someone cares enough about you to be kind. Don't tell me you never liked this?' his other hand on my jeans.

'In the past, you'd hurt me.'

'Not anymore,' rubbing me, breathing his scent into me, 'if you want someone to like you, you have to be nice to them,' he is bewitching me, 'let yourself enjoy them, enjoy yourself.'

'I am enjoying it, can't you feel the erection?' and for the first time in my entire life he bends over and gives me the blow-job that I've never been able to ask for. Almost instant relief and I'm glad, ashamed, embarrassed. He holds my red face and gently guides me to lie down and covers me with his jacket to sleep, tucking me in. Always knowing the right thing to do.

Toby

I wake early with a stiff neck after a cruddy night, kept awake half the time listening to himself jerking and yelping in his sleep. I couldn't put up with that. I take a breakfast tray upstairs, leave a cup of tea on Cally's locker and return quietly to sit on Andi's bed, watching her come-to in the curtained half-light. She unfurls and stretches tautness into her top.

'At least you've no black eyes,' she says, looking into mine.

'You heard us?'

'Hard not to. What were you fighting about?'

'We were just discussing things.'

'That loud? I don't think so.'

'Nothing for you to be concerned about. Anymore,' and I kiss her on the cheek and tiptoe back down through the quiet house and out the back door.

There are freshly dug piles of earth on the lawn. My dog or theirs?

Uncle Brown used to keep the pitch well manicured, free from any piles of earth dug up by the neighborhood dogs overnight. In between matches and in between our matches he'd scrape up the soil and, with a sick sense of balance, throw it down the rabbit holes that were pocking the grass and catching the players' feet. The following day the rabbits would have made more burrows and the dogs more mounds to fill them with. It was a relentless task. The horticultural experts fresh out of the pub, cutting past the pitch on their way home, would tell him it was moles causing the problem and he eventually got the idea of sticking an electric current down to kill them off. It might have done him out of a job. Instead his electric rod hit a power line and it did him out of his life. If only he'd have checked. There aren't even any moles in Ireland. How stupid some people can be. No joy in his ignorance. A just end to his war against the underworld.

There are no moles inside Cassie's mounds either. She's decorated some of them with twigs and dried leaves, others with the white pebble-dash she's picked off the walls. She made me dig one for her once, for a dead crow she wanted buried and was too scared to touch. Its angry family circling overhead, squawking their discontent. After the funeral she overcame her fear and dug it up again 'just in case he's still alive,' she said, and left it out on the wall for its friends to take away. The neighbour's cat did. You don't know what you'd find if you took a shovel to any of these. It's just her thing. At least hers are on the outside. I take a rusted spade left rotting at the side gate and raise it high above my head to strike one of the brown-mounded hides. Flattening my uncle with a whack so he stops. But finding it's too dense to level in one squash. It's a Picnic at Hanging Rock, holding the dead memories and sounds of the past. There's a whole fucking village of us here, living underground. Under the un-cut grass because Louis won't go near it. Hates the smell, it gets up his nose and explodes. Easy excuse for the lazy. Said the lady. Taking one for him up the arse and thanking Mr Brown for teaching our town how to do it.

I smash them all.

Cally

If Toby would just have a smoke it wouldn't look so bad, it's indecent to be outside this early in the morning. And all that thrashing around with a spade. Whatever will the neighbours think? What with their hedges cut low enough to see over and sweeping their leaves under the grass to rot away under the tidiness. Are they watching through their sparkling windows or are they peering out through the grime from under tatty scalloped blinds, passing judgement on the third person in this marriage? 'It's crowded,' the princess said. Will he stay here indefinitely and slowly push me out or will his presence be the glue that keeps us all together? Not everything should be resolved. He sees me and comes in, brushing the cold off himself. It smells fresh. Louis has put The Café Orchestra on and its lilting tunes have Toby swinging around in imaginary slow waltzes. He twirls towards me and places his hand in the small of my back to lead me around the kitchen. He skillfully guides my body to move in unison with his and I find he is gliding me over the surface of the floor, pulling me in closer until our bodies move as one. His inflections ripple through me, becoming not just a dance but a flow of sexual energy from his body into mine. The music is quickening, he is pulsing it through me, intense and in time. I feel the orgasm of the crescendo about to peak when Louis marches in.

'No. You're not doing that dancing with her.'

How come he knows this dancing? How come we've never danced like this? We separate in silent guilt.

'We were only dancing,' I say, for which I get a slap across the face.

'Slag. You and Andi, you're as bad as each other. Can't keep your hands off him, can you?'

'Andi? What do you mean Andi?'

'Yeah, you're not the only one. Don't think you're anything special.'

Turning to Toby now, I ask him what Louis meant by that, what did he and Andi get up to? He just shrugs and I charge upstairs, shouting her name to ask her myself. Not in bed. Her wardrobe door moves.

'What? You think you can get away with it by playing hide and seek like your kid sister? This is the grown up world you're meddling in now my girl and there are grown up consequences when you start messing around in it. Get out,' I pull the pretend wings off her that she thinks will somehow save her. Trying to look like Psyche when all she is, is mortal. She'll rue the beauty that is not hers, 'you are Andromeda!' I insist, yanking her out of her hiding place. Falling out with her tumble all the old boxes she has stashed at the bottom of it, their contents spilling into the angry room, 'what did you do to Uncle Toby? What have you done?' she is ignoring me, picking up her stuff, 'stop it. Look at me,' she is ferreting about, fretting over the ipods and cameras and spotlights and garters and what the hell is all this shit it's like a porn shop in here and it's in my little girl's wardrobe? She is frantically trying to box it all up but she can't take back what I have seen. Instead she has taken the force out of me. I am limping again, 'where did you get all this stuff?' I whisper at the growing misfortune.

'It's mine. Toby gave it to me.'

'It's Uncle Toby to you. Not all of it?'

'Yes.'

She is still scrabbling to hide it inside the dark floor of the cupboard, but it just won't fit anymore.

'There's so much. When?' picking the ipod out of a box, 'none of it's cheap. Why didn't we know about any of this? Why have you hidden it away? Why these things?' dangling a silver love-heart locket tangled up in some frilly underwear, 'these are for fifty year olds who can't get it up, not young teenagers.'

'He just wants me to have nice stuff. That's what people who love each other do.'

'Love each other? He's your uncle, not your boyfriend. You don't have sex with him,' she raises her eyebrows at me in insolence and I know. I know all the times he babysat, all the times he handed her a can of beer on the side, all the times he gave her lifts and brought her home late and put himself out for her and I know, he was doing her all the time, 'the fucking bastard,' I scream to all the bloody neighbours, to all the world, to all the fucking men who ever existed. Who the fuck would do this to a child? 'Louis, Toby, Uncle Brown,' I yell down the stairs, 'you're all the fucking same, groundsmen grinding away in your dirty huts! You broke my little girl,' smashing the studio spotlight off the landing, 'she was the most beautiful thing in the world,' I run backwards and forwards, lobbing my disgust down the stairs at them as Andi is crouched sobbing my pain and hers all over the emptying boxes. I can't shout it all out. I can't get it all out. It's too big and loud, a canyon too vast to expunge in one lifetime. Yet still I hear a noise coming out of me and still it keeps on coming and it is not enough. Nothing will ever be enough to release this planet of primal pain cutting out my womb.

Cassie

I didn't like seeing the octopus thingy. It's not the way my octopus is. It was shape-shifting and sliding into monster frightening. I didn't like being. In a room with it. Blackie ran down into the castle and held the keys of the jail. Prison Dog. It was full of cannibals and he was the boss of it. For a while. He had to stay here all night. He wakes up on the floor. There is war in my miniature houses and craters in the gardens. Uncle Toby on the inside, Uncle Toby on the outside. Blackie sees him do it. We are all smashed up, so I go outside to fix it. I want to re-bury the scary. I want to bury the shouty, the banging, the screaming and throwing. Me and Blackie pick up lots of broken stick insects. They got blasted. They are just potatoes really, sticks and bits of tin foil. They didn't stop the groundsman when he was kicking and whacking my cairns and his dog is just so stupid, not like Blackie. They always let the bad things come back out. So much mud in all the wrong places. I put a cannibal's head on one of the sticks. That should do it. And wave around some magic.

Louis

Toby leaves in a hurry, taking his dog with him, and Cassie the black dog is still moving her molehills to another part of the garden. I begin to clear up the broken gifts in the hallway. Each piece is thoughtful and I wish I'd thought of that. Such a waste. I cram the remains into the bin and work my way up the stairs, sweeping it all away. The moaning on the landing hasn't stopped, but at least the racket has. We were all stunned into silence by the force of Cally's outburst. It's hanging in the air like cordite and we are in shock that she even had a verbal Kalashnikov. It's new and heavy and we don't know how to dodge it. I walk around her while she rocks herself into a ball and Andi, I think from the sound of muted crying, is curled up back in the wardrobe. The boxes are empty now and I flatten them one by one in silence, lest the noise of our disaster opens up again, and carry them down to the recycling. I press the objects of our family meltdown further into the bin as if they are still in danger of escaping. Cassie is tiptoeing over the cracks in the patio. A message comes in from Sandy from sales. I thought I'd left all that behind me. Sounds urgent. Call me.

Wish I fecking didn't. Get her information. But she'd thought of me at least. I had to give her that even if I never got to give her the other. But she'd thought of me all the same. Didn't have to. I didn't want to hear what she'd said. Wish in time for a cup of tea, wishing for miracles. Nothing that a Barry's can't sort out, Mam would say to me. When a cup of tea would draw the line between Cally and me and let us start again. What with Sandy's news and Cally's behaviour, I have to start boiling the kettle. It heats up but I don't make that move with the cup. It feels too soon after all that drama and not quite right and I don't know when it will feel okay. Nothing feels okay. The scales itch away at my hands. I keep scratching, lifting my hands in supplication, weeping sores. It all comes out. No dressings. Therefore with angels and archangels and all the company of heaven above adore me, so I give them unto you Lord to do with as Thy will. Please don't. Let the police. In. On me. They asked Sandy questions. Thanks be to God she's no good at answering Mastermind. But I mind.

I have to sit for ten minutes before I can try again to make tea. The kettle boils quicker this time but it still doesn't feel ready. I wait. But I'm in a hurry. I have to turn it on every ten minutes in the hope that it will feel right then.

It doesn't. Nothing does. Was it 8.57? Is it 'T' for tip-off? Was it Sandy or HR Christine? Should I start the boil on the stroke of a ten minute sector, or at thirty four seconds prior to this? For ease of counting? I try both. The first way is easier. Just after I start boiling at 10.50 Cassie whips in through the door and gets off her muddied knees to tell me something. I'm too busy counting to listen. She distracts me and I have to count backwards to find the place in time that I forgot. She places her hand over mine and holds it there, stopping me from finding it.

'You don't have to do this Daddy,' she says.

But I do. She knows.

It's 10.50 and eighteen seconds. At 11.01 and eight seconds I boil. Not ready. At 11.11 and forty two seconds I boil again. It gets nearer to being easier to make a cup of tea, adding water on the go. Fifty three minutes later I make a cup and take it into our bedroom.

The locker is full of old mugs, books and Mogadons.

'You should only take these at night, then you'd be able to wash these up,' lazy. She stretches her arm out, eyes closed, waiting for me to put it in her hand.

'They're for my nerves.'

'There's nothing wrong with your nerves, you're quick enough to spot a tea.'

She rolls away, ignoring the effort that went into making this, rejecting my peace offering. I smash it onto the china-filled table-top.

The clumsy cow puts her hands into the mess of wet

shards to rescue her rescue pills.

'Looks familiar does it, like the crap you threw down the stairs? Think that's okay do you, to leave us to cut our feet off and expect the rest of the world to clean up after you? Yeah that's right, ignore me. Here, take the tablets. All of them. Take them all now and do us a favour, why don't you?'

'Oh God,' she moans.

'What? What exactly have you got to feel sorry for yourself? Nothing's happened to you.'

'Andi...' eyes still closed. I want to slap her awake.

'Oh get over it yourself. It was nothing. That man has done more to raise your daughter than you ever did. If you don't like it then start being a mother to her. And a wife to me. There is more important stuff going on.'

She's too far gone on her pills to care, or to take the bait to bite me back to give me the excuse I need to rip her up by her hair and grind her face in the broken cups until she realizes what a waste of space she is. I need her to do as she's told, not this medicated haze of indifference. She has to beg my forgiveness and show it on her knees, 'get down and pray,' I try to pull her out of her foetal position, but can't move her dead weight, 'just do it before you make me really annoyed,' she's heavy and limp, making me harder. I spoon in behind her and ram myself. She pulls away on purpose so I have to grip her. My right, 'look what you made me do,' and I hate her for what she just did, and I hate her for misbehaving on the stairs and for being useless and for chucking me out and for making it all about her when all this is happening. And her crying just makes me hate her even more, 'if you don't want any more then you have to stop crying,' she continues so she wants it. I oblige by striking her hard across her bare backside which is so disgusting I have to hit it again and again for being so vile until it stops wobbling and is hard and red so I stroke her gently, teasing the tease. She still does nothing for me. I look at the marks on her ass.

'Tell me you like it,' I tell her, 'tell me you want to put on your white socks and pull up your skirt in the city centre,' she needs to be kneed in the chest to answer. Making me do it, she is.

'I want all the strangers to look. Then an old man will come over to me,' Cally says.

'Good, you dirty slut. Then what?'

'He'll put it in my mouth.'

'And you're not wearing any panties?'

'No.'

'Why not?'

'I'm a dirty slut.'

'Yes. And what else are you wearing?'

'White socks.'

'What do you want?'

'You.'

'Good girl. He shuts you up with this does he?' and I pull her head around and push it in her face. Asking for it, she is. Uncle Brown tells me to.

But I have to react. Can't ignore what's happening and I head downstairs to look after it. I jump the bottom three steps in anger at what she makes me do. It's a jump too far and I stumble as my ankles give way and I tumble on the floor. I lie in expectation of being broken and in the stillness of the moment I hear her moving upstairs. She is waking and taking a shower to wash away her sins. Andi is moving about too, out of the wardrobe and ready to commit some more. How to control them? Mother, daughter, whores. Their fawning scrawning faces when they realize the threat of due processes and nonsense that could be coming down the line and what about the dread when she makes a show of herself in the papers? She'll lose the run of herself if I get arrested. Can't live without me, can't get rid of me. She tried but her betrayal failed with those vultures feeding on female fantasies of emancipated panties. Follow that up with a court case and laugh.

'She's withdrawn from the process, because she made up some nonsense.'

'Thank you for that clarification,' in your imagination. Of nerves. Seriously doing mine in, she is. Oh to escape her again. Get away from the naughtiness, the smacking and the sending to bed. All those grumbling girlies. My face is on the carpet. I turn my head sideways. A low-lying angle for supervising families. The canine Cassie is watching TV, blanking me out with the headphones on. I watch her through the doorway, sitting on her plastic chair. Sitting so solid, so dark. She shouldn't even be there, watching everything.

'What were you trying to say to me earlier?' I sit up on the stair, throwing a shoe which lands near her feet. Come to attention. Come the sergeants! Cum anywhere.

'Uncle Toby and his dog dug up my garden. Everything escaped.'

Except me. She is sinking, I am thinking, and I see her everywhere. Everything she sees. Uncles of dogness and deadness down there. She is sliding out secrets. All those sins and their sizzling stares. She is turning black and cuboid, shiny and made of heavy metal. There is a downward force pushing her into the ground and three thin wires connect her to each of us, taut like Uncle Brown's new goal nets straining to keep us in. I travel up the lines to two more rectangular anthracite boxes, so weighted they might push through the ceiling and come crashing down on top of me at any moment. Structurally the house isn't built for this, the floor loadings can't be sufficient. Not with the wooden hut's old planks, dusty and wanting. What if one of the cables snaps and whips my limb off in its recoil? Or pulls me down with them as they are dragged lower by their magnetic pull? The floorboards are already creaking under the strain. The block in front of me is slowly reeling us in, shortening and tightening the steel threads. If they were made of spider silk they would be five times stronger, but she would eat me and I'm already being eaten alive as it is. I have to know their density, are they strong enough? But it's black and I don't have time to work it all out before it breaks. Why can't everything be stable? It's too much information at once. I have to prise my family out of this force-field of decay.

'I have to go out,' I shout over the electron din.

Cally

Andi has gone to school breakfast club and I haven't even started on Cassie when the doorbell starts ringing. Great timing, don't think I'm going to be answering doors to strangers first thing in the morning. And Louis has been gone all night. Is it Friday? If they know me they would have phoned first, or shouted 'hya' through the letterbox knowing I'd be resting. Only scammers and carpet sellers or those nosey tyrants from the census come knocking on doors. As well as the Jehovah's, but they're made to do that or they'll go to Hell. They're going there anyway. So you should let them in and tell them what they've got isn't real. They need a proper church like the rest of us, even if we haven't been there since 1980. Apart from births, marriages, deaths and First Communions, obviously. Got to have a backup plan just in case we got it wrong for the last few decades and there is an actual God up there who'll give-out to us for skiving off from the boring bits every Sunday morning. I haven't been struck down yet. The Jehovah's are getting persistent at the door, desperate for their salvation through mine. As I open it on the chain a great hand tries to shove itself in and a voice says I have to facilitate entry they have a warrant to search the premises and shouting and all and I've no idea what he's on about and I can hear the back door being rattled and bodies coming in and a load of rushing and,

'Please will someone just tell me what's going on?' as a paper is flashed in front of me, as if that explains anything and they are all over the place like navy ants. Up and down the stairs and bellowing instructions about what, I don't know. Some gurrier stops and takes the mobile out of my hand with his rubber gloves on and I ask him if there's a virus and he says,

'You could say that.'

I cover my nose and he makes me sit on the sofa and stands over me and pushes me back down when I try to stop some sergeant who's going through my drawer of memories, flinging things out onto the floor like a burglar.

'This is how it's meant to look before you lot get called in, not after,' I say and the man says he knows it's difficult with private stuff but it has to be done, 'but what for? If you'd just tell me what's going on?'

'How many digital media items are in the house' he asks and I haven't a clue what he means by that.

'Laptops, tablets, touch screens, mobiles, Wiis, Xboxes.'

'I don't know', and I don't

'What have I done? What's my house done?' they have a human chain handing transparent plastic bags of our stuff down the stairs. Jesus, everyone will see, 'will you be bringing those things back?' no answer, 'because I don't want those bags of broken yokes you're carrying out,' all the electrical things Louis never got around to fixing. Says he keeps them just in case he needs a spare hard drive or modem or whatever those green boards are called, 'they don't even work, they just fill up the bedroom floor. Take as many as you like. Doing me a favour,' I shout into the hall, 'Jesus, will someone please tell me what's going on?'

They leave just as quickly as they came and Louis is nowhere to sort it out. The mess is something else. Idiot for opening the door, for leaving the back unlocked. There are bits of Andi's babyhood smeared over the wooden floor by their strange and angry boots and her little wrist band from the maternity hospital has been flattened. I kept it for the hole in the middle, for the shape left by her tiny two day old hand. Now it's destroyed with the space of her presence removed. I don't give a shit about the mess but this guts me, pulling a baby's arm out of its past. And for what? A bunch of cruddy computer parts. My hands are shaking and I can hardly think my ears are pumping so loud. A woman sits next to me. Why not invite the entire estate in to have a gawk while you're at it? She says she is here to talk, family liaison. But we don't need any counselling, liaising. None of that. She clarifies, she thinks, but not the chaos surrounding me.

'You can speak now,' she says.

I tell her I have to tidy up. Would you look at it? Who the hell did they think they were?

'Those were genuine officers, with warrants,' she is nicer than they were, trying to explain, 'I'll be with you throughout the process.'

But stuff is everywhere and she is making a process of making tea in my kitchen and asking about my Louis and I'd like to know where Louis is but it's all I can do to find us the mugs. Next she'll be telling social workers that I can't keep the place clean.

'I'll stay with you to help you through it,' she says.

Fat help she'll be as she steps over the sprawl on the floor like I always store my teaspoons on the lino. She wants to talk a bit more, she says, but I don't have any Flash left or Mr Sheen. Too much shining and she is doing my head in.

'Do you understand?' she asks.

I don't, so I tell her I do, perhaps she will go.

'Good.'

But she doesn't leave. Ages and ages and the haywire is in front of me and inside me. I stare at it, waiting for her to leave. She waits for my answers. I begin collecting the bits of my children off the floor and wrap them in some extra love to put away for another twenty years. I work my way around the room and onto the next one, restoring the little histories that have been torn from their nests. She is following me everywhere, like a toddler. I zone-out until there is just noise coming from her mouth and sure what can you do about that? I have an audience on my shoulder for the things I am finding. Discoveries of things I didn't even know we had. Some of it hasn't been out since we moved here, some of it dating back to our parents' houses. And she's in our histories now, prying as she's trying to get more out. They had lifted boxes down from the attic to rummage through and I find my mum's set of oriental china she never used, it was kept for best, and the sherry glasses too small for a decent drink, too fragile for a shot glass. She was a gin drinker anyway so you wouldn't smell it on her breath. Like you couldn't tell. They've ripped the back off her antique mirror, destroying it and for what? It was no use as a mirror it was so old, but I saw her every time I passed it with her hair setting under a scarf and putting on her coral lipstick for stepping out the door. They've taken that away from me. Andi's carpet was a kip anyway, I'll leave that to her. Cassie tiptoes around it all, afraid she'll stand on bits of one of us. Or she's oblivious to it and is just doing her funny walk, being a kid. She was sat staring at the floor the whole time the raid was on as if it wasn't even happening. I wish I could be more like that. Her sister is home and the woman still glued to my back.

'I'll give you two a few minutes to explain,' she explains, 'while I report back.'

She steps out to the garden. Jesus, that bomb-site,

and is straight on her job.
    'Social worker?' Andi asks.
    Why not? A text comes. I act.

Andi

'We're going to Bray,' Mum tells us.

That's twice in a lifetime. What's wrong with her, proving herself to the one outside?

'Yeeah,' Cassie runs her delight around in circles.

'Shhh, to have a picnic on the hill,' she says, 'but only if you're really quiet. Remember Proteus?'

Jesus.

'The beach,' Cassie wishes.

'No, a hike. Too dangerous for sitting down. And cold,' she has to ruin it.

She starts getting all impatient with herself . I don't wink at Cassie or say it'll be fun because it won't. It'll be mega boring and we don't have walking boots. It will be dark at this rate.

'You too,' Mum says to me.

'Like fuck.'

'In,' and I know she means it.

'Somewhere nice to get out,' her version of persuasion, 'make an effort,' getting at me, 'get your coat,' she orders and I don't, 'hurry,' she takes me aside, 'just play along with it will you?' I always do, 'it's that woman outside,' she grinds through her teeth.

'What about your woman?'

'What's she doing?'

'On the phone.'

'Good let's get going.'

Cassie gets bundled into the car. Dressed up for a carnival in her tutu with knee-high socks, wellies, rabbit ears and the butterfly wings. She is wielding a walking stick with a decapitated Barbie head stuck on top of it. I say she's too cute to cover up, apart from the barmy baton, but she insists Barbie's been better that way since her body went missing. I have to agree until she puts it in her mouth and then mum really should intervene. We are only ten minutes down the road when she stops for Dad. They have a chin-wag out on the pavement. For, like, ever. Cassie is going mental.

'Can we go home now?' I ask.

No. They get in, with Dad taking over the driving. Effing great. Stuck on a family outing. Cassie is banging the back of his seat like a nut-job. He tells us to stop fighting there in the back and we look behind at whoever he thinks is at war in his world. He slams on the brakes and yells at us, pulling our necks and the steering wheel out of joint.

I notice the ring I found outside is back on his wedding finger and I would've been pleased if he wasn't being such a prick right now, or then, or ever. We ignore him until he gets distracted by his road rage and we can mimic him going purple and keeling over. He torments us by driving past the nice bit of Bray with the beach and promenade and the candy floss. Too tight to get an ice-cream. He drives for ages away from the town and into the countryside, stopping at some field on the other side of the big rocky hill with a cross on top of it. It really is going to be a hike.

'We came here once before,' Mum says.

'And you came back? Incredible,' I say.

'I don't want to go to the crackling field,' Cassie says, 'it's a noisy yellow field.'

'How can it make a noise?' Dad asks.

'In the summer it was making sounds, like it was snapping. I don't want to go in there again.'

God he is getting exasperated,

'It won't be making any noise now. Come on get out all of you. Where's the Queen?'

'Just getting your stuff,' Mum answers.

Why not bow to him while you are at it?

'Which of you is the Queen?' I ask.

'You mean the Queen Mother?' Mum tries to sacrifice herself.

'Ha. Well it couldn't be me now could it?' Dad assumes. But we know otherwise. Say nothing lest Dad has an epiphany about it all over again.

Cassie

Walk through the fields. See the hill ahead. Tramping. Hear that crunchy barley stubble I remember from when it was summer here and I heard it crackling in the hot sun. Bits of that smell hanging around in today. It's coming up from the ground, from the frozen mud. Even the crows are quiet. It is late afternoon. The sky is a weird bright blue, like in the photos. And it is very still, like the solar eclipse was, Daddy says. It will be sunset soon. Daddy is leading us all in a straight line through the long dead grass with cutty scratchy things in it. Flicking back on my legs. Got to climb over them. Piles of rocks and stones. Tidy farmers. They made this hill by putting all their rocks on it. And little stones getting in the way. Each time stacking them up in the one place, out of the way. Now it's really in the way. A big, steep, mountainy climb. Rock-hard grey. I put some of the smaller stones in my pocket for all the holes I have to dig in our garden, really big ones for our bin and our floor and our upstairs. It will take days. Even Blackie will get tired of it, but it has to be done. Uncle Toby could help me. He owes me for all the ones he broke. And then he can dig his own. I finger the gravel. And scramble and clamber up the biggest cairn ever, feet stamping it down, pressing it all back in. It's all around me. I'd make a good groundsman, Daddy always tells me. He is one. I'm still practicing. It's very steep. And we're all puffing and I look up and the light is just melting away. No special sunset, the sun just snuck off slowly so we didn't notice it going. I hurry up and I'm the first to reach the tiny flat bit at the top.

'I win. I can see everything,' all the sky with my head right back. Dance and keep my head right back, only backwards. Sharp sounds, sharp like a bang and a pop, and I crouch to shift into Blackie.

I go round and round and round and round and round and round and round and round I go, chasing my tail and getting dizzy and more and more. Clatter of crows can you hear me? Squawkers. Lots of squawkers. Bird alert, 'answer me birds and tell me what you're saying,' Daddy bird flying the loudest. Daddy bird upside down and black eyes and poky beaky black. Round and round. Squawking. All crashing and flapping. Dizzy and round and round. Poky beaky poking squawking. Stop them if I can squawk and flap the loudest. Flappy birds black beak sharp in Andi's neck. Red and her tummy all raging red. And round. Squawky flappy beaky daddy bloody Andi. Stop it, I bite your leg then get kicked off so I lick my Andi bird. My Andi. Looking for Mammy bird to save her but Mammy bird has crashed too. No flapping. No squawking. Just black eyes looking up. I look up too to the black sky. I can see Andi in the sky, just like she said.

Acknowledgments

Sean, my editor, for all his coaxing and ego-strokes and for pulling a blinder which is this book.

Chris, for all his work in making things work at époque press.

Wordsmiths Writers Group for enduring my insufferable self as I learn to write.

Jessie for putting-up with me all these years when no-one else would.

And finally, my family who lived in a pigsty throughout the editorial process. And didn't even notice.